INFURIATED

MAYA DANIELS

Vinci Books

vinci-books.com

Published by Vinci Books Ltd in 2026

1

The EU GPSR authorised representative is Logos Europe, 9 rue Nicolas Poussion, 17000 La Rochelle, France
contact@logoseurope.eu

By Maya Daniels

Daywalker Series

Investigated

Infiltrated

Instigated

Initiated

Infuriated

Ignited

Chapter One

"Drake! Your ass better be awake!"

Jolted out of a fitful sleep by the shout, my legs scissor and tangle in the sheets. I kick something heavy, and it jerks away when I kick it. Whatever it is, it shifts to the left of the bed, the mattress dipping low enough to roll me to my side until I collide with a thick, warm body full of muscle. My mind is stuck between the weird dreams that have been on loop every night and the momentary panic knowing someone is inside my place, although I can't recall which place it is. An engine rumbles, picking up in volume somewhere outside. Seeing only darkness in front of my eyes, I blink owlishly to try to clear my vision.

The darkness shifts in my face.

With a shriek, I shove away from it, but I misjudge the strength I put behind my push and end up wind-milling my arms for a long second before I land hard on the floor, bruising my tailbone as my naked ass slaps on the parquet. The springs on the metal frame protest and squeak when a huge black head with piercing emerald eyes peeks down at me from the top of the bed. Tenebris smirks, and that stupid gaze of his travels over my naked body sprawled on the ground. In this moment, I realize it wasn't an engine that I heard. It was him purring next to me. He must have snuck in again in the middle of the night and crawled in beside me, and he had to have known I'd be angry about it the moment I woke up.

"Drake!"

The banging of cabinets and the tinkling of ceramic mugs comes from the kitchen down the hall, followed by too-loud grumbling and cursing. Ignoring the damn panther and the frustrated muttering of the intruder, my head moves slowly as I look around the room, my eyes stopping at the slightly-parted curtains on the window where a barely-there light from the approaching dawn is struggling to be seen. The sight of the familiar place I've called home in the last week slows the thundering in my chest and calms the magic pulsing with its own beat between my breasts, which allows me to finally take a full breath and release it slowly.

"Oh good, you're up." Tucking my legs under me, I jump to my feet and face Myst. "I was going to drag you out of bed by your feet."

She'll do it, too. As a matter of fact, she has done it twice so far. The second time she barely escaped Tenebris's teeth, which were an inch from her face. My eyes flick from her to the panther and he cocks his head to the side, his right ear swiveling like a satellite dish while he eyes Myst contemplatively. I wonder if he is thinking the same.

"Don't even think about it." Pulling the teaspoon out of her mouth—she went after the peanut butter again even though I hid the damn jar—Myst stabs the air with it, pointing it from the panther's face to mine. "I'll neuter him

2

and stab you in the boob with this spoon before either of you move."

"Why are you here at this ungodly hour, Myst?" Jamming my fists on my hips, I glare at her as I try to ignore the fact that I'm butt naked and Tenebris is giving me side-eyed glances. "And have you heard of knocking? It's what normal people do instead of breaking into someone's home."

"We"—She twirls the spoon in the air between us, grinning like a fiend— "are neither normal people, nor is this your home. It's mine, and I let you stay here. And that brings me to the reason I'm here at this ungodly hour, as you so eloquently put it. He is getting to be the biggest pain in my ass, and I've had a lot of pains in my ass, trust me. It says a lot about the situation."

'What are you talking about?"

I can't help but wonder if the female is losing her mind. Myst always acts a little unhinged, which keeps anyone around her wary and on their toes. She is muttering under her breath even now as she scowls at her feet. I have a hard time figuring out what version is the real her and which one she uses to keep people away from her, to be honest. And they say I'm weird and unstable.

"I've managed to keep us hidden, even against the added efforts he has put into his search, but there's no denying the fact that he is pulling out the big guns. Looking at you like this, I can't say I blame him, but enough is enough." Her chocolate eyes lift to my face and darken to swirling shadows. Black mist covers the whites, and the effect curdles my blood. "If he sends that arrogant jerk my way, I'm going to slaughter you all." She blinks once and the darkness disappears like it was never there, the switch in her attitude almost giving me whiplash. A bright smile blossoms on her face. "You look like you need coffee, Chicca. Good thing I started the brewer. Hurry up and get dressed because we have things to do."

With that, she claps her hands happily, spins around, and vanishes in the hall leaving me staring at the empty doorway with my jaw hanging to my chest. Lifting my gaze to Tenebris, he looks as confused as I feel. He even shakes his head sharply while rubbing a plate-sized paw over his head twice, his tail twitching limply behind him.

"This is going to be a shitty day. I can feel it." I rub my forehead, releasing a heavy sigh that feels like it's torn all the way from my toes.

"We don't have all day!" Myst yells from the kitchen, the banging even louder than before. It makes me wonder if she's looking for something or if she's just making noise to piss me off.

Snatching the clothing that's draped over a chair in the corner of the bedroom, I stab my legs in the jeans angrily. Being around this female takes some getting used to. I'm not sure if it's just me, but her mood affects my emotions. She has a tendency to sweep in like a tornado, taking you on a wild ride that leaves you dazed when it ends.

Anger and rage have been a constant companion of mine since the Board knowingly—or unknowingly for that matter—forced me to kill my own brother. I didn't know the male, never knew I had a sibling even though I've seen him twice, though the second time he was unconscious with machines connected to his body. But he was mine. He was blood and they took him from me. What they did made them as bad as Roberti, if not worse, but either way they definitely earned a place on my shit list. My hatred for all of them burns in my veins day and night, but it gets overwhelming when Myst is in one of her moods. I can't think of anything but bloodlust ... like right now.

Tugging a long-sleeved shirt over my head, I pad bare-foot down the hall on silent feet. Tenebris is right on my heels, the heat of his body warming the back of my thighs even when I don't hear him move. Silent death I call him in my head. The panther is a sneaky little shit. Typical cat. An asshole like a cat, too.

"There you are." Myst plants a mug in my hands, wrap-ping my fingers around it and giving me a squeeze until she is sure I won't drop it. "Drink up."

Plopping on the high chair by the kitchen island, I lean my elbows on the counter and cradle the mug. The steam is fogging Myst's features even as it swirls under my nose like a siren song, so I blow on it before taking a sip. I'm not a big coffee drinker, preferring a good tea over the vile dirt water, but on days like this I welcome the kick it'll give me.

"Let's start from the beginning." Gingerly, I set the mug down before it burns the palms of my hands. The coffee is unsweetened and black like my soul ... or maybe hers. It's a toss-up between the two of us, honestly. "Who pissed you off so much that you showed up here a couple of hours before you normally would?"

I don't like morning people. They are chirpy, bright-eyed, and bushy-tailed at hours that even the devil himself wants to dig a hole and hide. It's unnatural, especially for my kind. We are creatures of the night, Daywalkers included. We should never be bright-eyed or bushy-tailed ... well, besides Tenebris, whose tail fluffs up in anger when he's ready to pounce.

"The powers are shifting. He will send the jerk to find me next just so he can get to you." Leaning a hip on the island across from me, she folds her arms under her breasts.

"It's not going to happen." Huffing in frustration, she glares at my coffee. "That's a low blow even for him."

"Who?" She jerks at my shout, but I can't help it. I'm at my wits end with her. "You might as well speak in a foreign language, Myst. I don't understand a word coming out of your mouth."

"Zoltan." Her voice is calm and flat.

My heart, on the other hand, jumps to the roof of my mouth, somersaulting between my throat and my chest before plummeting to my feet and splattering on the floor. Swaying on the chair, I grip the island tightly with my fingers so I don't fall off it, bright spots dancing at the edges of my vision. Tenebris chirps, bumping his head on my leg to get my attention. It is just what I need to pull me out of the panic threatening to suffocate me. Prying my fingers off the edge of the counter, which I'm clutching with a white-knuckled grip, I sink them into his fur and ground myself to his solid presence.

"We need to hide." Pushing the words through numb lips, my nostrils flare as I take control of my unsteady breathing.

I don't want to see Zoltan. Not now, and not until I have killed every single one of the ones who thought it'd be fun to play games with my life, every single one of them who thought they could take control of my actions to make me a puppet in their game. The vampire will want to take me back to the academy because in his head that's my home, so that's where I belong. He couldn't be more wrong, but I don't have the energy to explain it to him, nor do I want to.

"I will make sure he doesn't find you if that's what you want." Tilting her head to the side, Myst watches me with a knowing look. It's plain as day that she understands exactly how I feel, and I have a feeling Fenrir is the reason.

What a fucking mess.

"I don't want to see any of them." Swallowing thickly, I scrape my nails over Tenebris's head and shoulders, his purr growing louder by the second. "Not yet." Myst flicks her gaze to the panther, and when she turns to me again her eyebrow is cocked like an arrow. "If you showed up sooner, he wouldn't be here either. I had no choice but to let him come along."

"Sometimes, Chicca, I wonder if you believe the lies you tell everyone or if you're simply so naïve that think you are telling the truth."

"I don't need a therapist, Myst." Snatching the mug off the island, the hot liquid sloshes over my hand and burns my skin. I don't wipe it, instead relishing in the pain because it takes my mind off other things. Tightening my hold, I chug half of the scolding coffee, daring her to say a word by not looking away from her face. "I need to find Roberti and end this once and for all."

"Mhmm." Her eyes narrow slightly but she doesn't say anything, only lifts her own mug to her lips and sips the coffee as she watches me with her forehead scrunched in contemplation. "And you still need me for that because you are nowhere ready to walk among humans without bringing attention to yourself."

"I'm learning." I hate that I sound defensive because I'm more upset with myself than she'll ever be for taking this long to learn a simple parlor trick. "I'll try harder." When her lips twitch, my palm itches to slap her. "I'm paying you to help me."

"Which reminds me." Lowering her mug with a clunk, she regards me through a slanted gaze, suspicion oozing out of her every pore. "You promised a serpentine stone. One I have yet to see."

"I'm not lying to you. I have the stone; I just left it at a friend's place. You'll have it the moment I get it back. Trust me, I never go back on my word."

"You have a serpentine and you just leave it at a friend's place?" Her eyebrows almost disappear in her hairline. "Let's go back to my statement from earlier. I'm leaning more towards naïve right now."

"What's the big deal anyway?" Tossing back the remaining coffee, I slam the empty mug on the island. "It's a stupid rock."

Myst chokes on her tongue, and I swear Tenebris snickers.

"The damn thing almost killed me." Muttering under my breath, I jump off the chair.

"Say what now?" The sharp, intent look on her face chills me to the bone, and I regret not keeping my mouth shut.

"What's the plan?" Switching the subject, I stretch my arms above my head. I didn't sleep well at all. Again. Everything hurts and I'm more tired now than I was a few days ago.

Myst searches my face long enough to make me uncomfortable, so I shuffle my feet and force my hands to hang limply at my sides so I don't fidget. With effort, I keep my breathing even, pretending I don't notice how still Tenebris is next to me. Nothing living should be able to stay motionless like he does. Goosebumps pop up on my arms and legs.

"We continue practicing until it gets dark," she finally says, giving the panther a quick look. "Then we hunt for Roberti."

"Oh, joy!" My fake enthusiasm about practicing makes Myst grin.

I never want to see a chilling smile like that as long as I live.

Chapter Two

Wiping my sweaty palms off the jeans I'm wearing, I tug the hem of the bright pink t-shirt Myst made me wear. It has a stupid, sparkling rainbow and a freaking unicorn on it, too. If I didn't know better, I'd say she makes me dress in obnoxious colors to attract more attention, and to make it harder for me to control the effect I have on humans. Which is the total opposite of what I'm trying to achieve here, but when I mention it, she makes me feel stupid by telling me this is how humans dress and I need to blend in. Blend in my ass. Not a single person is dressed like me.

So, here I am, staring at the double doors of a large shopping mall like I'm facing a ruthless monster that will bite me the second I move. Chatter and white noise come every time the doors slide open and closed, the humans oblivious to the danger standing a few feet away at the curb dressed in a pink t-shirt. Instead, they go about their day with their faces shoved in their phones. They ignore me only because Myst cast some bubble around me when she kicked me out of the car with her boot like she was tossing out a bag of trash. Her tires squealed when she left, Tenebris hissing and growling in the back seat because she wouldn't let him join me. Like that's something else I need apart from this hideous t-shirt. Walking around this mall full of humans with a black panther twice the size of the regular animal, I know my face will be plastered on every news channel the humans have within minutes. Screw Roberti, Zoltan will be on me like white on rice within sixty seconds.

A shiver passes down my spine.

"It's now or never, Franky."

Blowing out a breath, I wipe my hands again. I'm sweating like a whore at church, my eyes darting left and right as if the humans can hurt me when it's definitely me they need to worry about. Chanting in my head that I'm a Daywalker now and they won't be able to feel what I am unless I want them to, my knee jerks up but my legs won't move. Since the initiation, I no longer need sunglasses. That took a few days to get used to. The first morning I watched the sunrise, I didn't blink. My eyes burned as tears soaked into the collar of my shirt. Not from pain, no. It was from the brightness and the beauty of it. A sunrise has so many colors, and it reminds me of my vision when the Dragon Blood takes over, though it's muted somewhat. It's still a sight to behold.

The horn of a vehicle blares loudly from the street at my back and jerks me out of my thoughts. I know I'm stalling, and when I look over my shoulder, my eyes land on someone else who knows it, too. My eyes lock on Myst, who's smirking at me through the windshield of the car she has parked across the street. Her elbow lifts and the horn blares again, which makes me realize she must have done it the first time also. Her grin grows, and I scowl at her, at least until a black head pops out between the seats. Tenebris looks pissed. His ears are flattened to the sides and his lips are curled in a snarl an inch from Myst's face. Her lips move, and whatever she says to him makes his eyes shoot my way. Luckily, he doesn't rip her throat out. This time. The panther looks as happy as a cat pulled out of a forced shower, but he doesn't attack and he doesn't move.

Flicking my braid over my shoulder, I face the mall again. I can do this. The sooner it's over, the faster I'll be able to find Roberti and make him pay. With that perspective at the front of my mind, I square my shoulders and take the first steps. The moment I move from the spot I'm standing in, the air around me ripples, the bubble Myst cast around me dissolving into nothingness. Like thousands of ants crawling over my body, I feel every eye in the place focus on me.

Keeping my gaze straight, I force my legs to move casually even when all I want to do is sprint inside and get the hell out as fast as I can. Short taps of a horn followed by a few cat calls echo around me, and unfortunately, they don't come from Myst this time. The short hairs escaping my braid dance around my face, the cool air-conditioning blasting me when I walk through the sliding glass doors.

The noise is louder inside, slightly disorienting for a moment until my hearing adjusts to it. People call out names, mingling with the excited shrieks of happiness and the screaming of infants until I have to force my hands to my sides so I don't cover my ears. Clenching my fists, I focus on pulling my energy as close to me as I can. It fights me, struggling like a living thing unwilling to obey me. The faces around me blur in my unseeing eyes, while I wrestle with it, doing my best to get it just under my skin. That's all I have to do to make this work, at least according to Myst.

"Holy shit, is this chick real?" a male voice says loudly

from my left, lust and hunger dripping from his words as he inches closer.

My feet speed up, the scuffing of my sneakers too loud to my ears. I'm still focused on dragging my energy to me, my teeth grinding hard from the effort. Beads of sweat sprinkle my forehead, yet it's still pulsing, luring its prey like a flame would a moth. *How do you control your own nature? Is it possible to go against what you are?* I push the voice away before it can make me doubt myself. I can do this. I know I can.

I'm starting to get claustrophobic from all the humans edging closer to me with their eyes glazed over and full of hunger. My skin is crawling with repulsion from seeing the effect we have on them. No wonder they were hunting us down and the Accord was signed to keep us away. For all his insanity, at least Roberti kept them safe by enforcing it. Until now. If I don't do this, who will protect them when the portals go down? And the question is not IF they will go down, but WHEN. Determination rushes through my veins like hot lava. Enough people have died. No more.

Like the loud snap of a rubber band, my energy slaps into place writhing under my skin. A soft sigh passes over the inside of the mall like a wave, and I curiously watch the humans shake their heads and move along with frowns on their faces. A smile lifts my lips, and when I stop walking it widens until I'm grinning like a fool.

I did it!

It feels like I'm about to split at the seams from the pressure inside me but no one is staring at me or preparing to grope me. Humans zero, Francesca one. I made it happen and I'm so proud of myself I can't stop grinning. Twirling in a circle, my smile slips into a grimace when I catch my reflection on the storefront. The damn pink t-shirt is an eyesore if I've ever seen one. Myst will eat her words when I swagger out of the mall.

"Hello beautiful." I stop turning in a circle to face the same human that wanted to know if I was real earlier.

Cocking my head to the side, I search his face, but his eyes are not glazed over so it's not my energy luring him to me. Hunger is still bright and clear though, and it sets all my instincts on alert. His hair is buzzed so short I can see his scalp under it. His face is rounded with a strong jaw, a slightly-corked nose sitting between hazel eyes and thick eyebrows. Since he is of average height and weight, he is no threat to me, but he will definitely be one to a human female. Judging by the leer on his face, he thinks I'm one of those too.

How sad for him.

"I haven't seen you around here before." He moves into my personal space like it's his right.

"And you know everyone in this place?" Lifting an eyebrow, I don't take a step back when he gets so close his chest almost touches mine.

"I make it my business to know everyone, especially a hot piece of ass like you." His stale breath washes over my face and I have to force myself not to gag. Or punch him.

"Quite a charmer, I see." Batting my eyelashes like an idiot, I give him a dumb smile. "Lucky me. You found me the second I stepped foot inside."

"It is your lucky day." His leer is sickening. "Come, let me show you around."

Without waiting for permission, he wraps his thick fingers around my upper arm and steers me towards a metal door to our right with a green-glowing exit sign above it. I don't fight him. I allow him to think he has the upper hand while using our skin-to-skin contact to read his emotions, though it does take a great amount of effort on my part. Bile rises in my throat at all the nasty thoughts floating through his mind. To make matters worse, this is not the first time he has done something like this: approached a female and muscled her to a place where he can do whatever he wants. A place where nobody will hear her scream or call for help. He glances at me and I smile as brightly as I can. Excitement courses through his body, and he shivers from it.

"You'll shiver soon enough, alright," I mumble under my breath through unmoving lips.

"What did you say hot stuff?" One meaty hand shoves the metal door open and he yanks me through it.

"You're strong." I breathe to sidetrack him, acting impressed by his manhandling.

His chest puffs up. "I am. You'll see how strong in a minute." He licks his lips while his eyes peruse my body from my head to my feet. "This way."

We enter a dimly-lit parking lot, the stench of gas fumes, oil leaks, and stale urine making me choke and gag while the human drags me behind him. Through the nausea, I wonder why he doesn't find it strange that I go with him without a protest. Human females can't be so gullible they'd let him get away with something like this. Thinking back, I realize it didn't take him more than a couple seconds to get me out of that door. He followed behind me, but he only approached when I neared the exit of the mall.

Sneaky, sneaky human.

The male leads us to a staircase, his steps filled with urgency. Deciding to make this more interesting, I dig my heels in, resisting his strength but not by much. No fun in tipping him off that he's bitten off more than he can chew this time. Acid fills my mouth when I see him adjusting himself, his erection tenting his jeans hanging below his ass. How he walks without tripping is beyond me.

"Now, now." He tightens his grip on my arm, and I know if I were human there'd be a bruise there. "We are almost there, then you can fight and scream as much as you like."

"It's the stupid t-shirt, isn't it?"

I look down at the sparkling rainbow tee, the horn of the unicorn nestled between my boobs. It's the only reason for any man to look at me and think it would be a good idea to take me somewhere that nobody will hear me scream. As Daren and Fenrir would say, I'm too prickly for anyone to think it is a good idea to approach me. My resting bitch face helps, too.

"Don't worry, I'll shred that abomination in a second." Huffing, he rushes down the metal stairs while dragging me with him. His boots clink with every hit, sounding like gunshots in the narrow space. The stench of urine and other feces is stronger here so I breathe through my mouth.

"I knew it! I told Myst it's horrible." At the mention of Myst, his head snaps in my direction, his gaze chilling and intent.

"Your friend was with you?" Stopping isn't a great idea because I'm about to hurl all over him from the stench.

"No, she just dropped me off." Moving past him, I'm now lugging him down the stairs with him clinging to my arm.

"You're an eager one, aren't you?" A manic look enters his gaze when I glance at him. "This way." Jerking me to a stop, he opens a door and pulls me out to a different level of the parking lot, this one with a hell of a less cars.

Moving with purpose, he leads me to a lone door between two brick pillars, and all I can think is how happy I am that the control I hold over my energy is still strong. I can't wait to see the look on Myst's face when she sees it. The human opens the door and a new scent coming from what looks like a maintenance closet churns my stomach. Desperation and sex. My heart slows to a crawl as all my senses are sharpening. There is enough space between the carts full of brooms, mops, and buckets of paint for the two of us to squeeze in.

Jerking my arm out of his grasp, I grab his shoulder and shove him inside. Cans hitting the concrete floor bounce in the tight space when he kicks them, slamming his hands on the wall so he doesn't introduce his face to it. I follow behind him, closing the door with a click. The darkness is pierced by an automatic yellow light that buzzes above our heads. My eyes flick around the place, the human too busy fumbling with the button of his jeans to notice me. He gives up on it, yanking them to his knees since they were already sagging from his ass. A leer is plastered on his face, making his average looks ugly.

My eyes lock on a yellow elastic band on the ground, a long chunk of blonde hair as thick as my forefinger still twisted around it. I already suspected it, but now I know for sure. He has done this to many women. Rage turns my vision red, and I can feel my eyes shifting. I still keep the control of my energy, but my power thrums out, writhing around the tight space. I close my eyes and bask in it.

"Get down on your knees." The human snarls as he grabs my braid and jerks my head up.

I open my eyes very slowly. The first thing I see is his erection, which is pointing my way and turning an angry red from the tight grip he has on it. My gaze travels up until we lock eyes. His widen, the blood draining from his face as he flinches back when I trip over his jeans and end up half-seated on the tipped-over buckets. A thick chain with a gold cross as big as my palm swings from his shirt, thumping against his chest.

"How about you get on your knees, human?" My smile grows wide enough to show him the tips of my fangs, and his mouth works in silent words, his eyes bulging out of their sockets. "And start praying to your God." My head tilts to the side, my braid swinging over my shoulder like a pendulum. "I must warn you. He will not listen. Not this time."

His death is too fast for my liking, his sour blood tasting more like chemicals than the fluid of life. Mindful not to cover myself in it, I turn him so his back is pressed to my chest, and after a second or two, I twist his neck and drop his lifeless corpse at my feet. The stench hits me again with a vengeance, this time mixed with the scent of his blood. I jerk the door open and stumble out of the tiny room, emptying my stomach to the side.

"Oh, dear fates, I killed him." The reality of what I did hits me like a rock on the back of my head. I hurl again.

"He deserved it."

I jump a foot off the ground when a voice comes from behind me.

Chapter Three

"Go away."

I can't even find the strength to freak out because Leo is here when I've done everything I could think of to avoid all of them. He creeped in silently, and I didn't even feel his presence until he spoke.

"You did good, Drake." The alpha sounds damn proud, which only pisses me off.

"Fuck you, mutt." Spitting the disgusting taste from my mouth, I wipe it with the back of my hand.

"I told you that you missed out on that, Drake. Real shame, but the fact you still want to is a statement of my greatness." He winks when I turn my glare on him, leaning his shoulder on one brick pillar.

Naked.

"You need to start wearing clothes, pup." Pressing my back on the wall behind me, I close my eyes and sigh. My legs can't carry my weight right now.

"And hide this?" The air stirs around us and I pop one eye open only to see him swirl his hand over his nakedness.

"Not a chance. It'd be the greatest sin committed against humanity."

"You're not human."

"Touché!" His boyish grin makes my lips twitch for a split second.

"Is Zoltan with you?"

I'm a killer. The thought is the only thing I can really focus on and it screams in my head so loud I can't even begin to worry about the vampire coming at me from some silent, dark corner.

"I might be loyal to him Drake, but stupid I am not." A dimple I've never noticed winks in his cheek. "I'll have to tell him that I found you, but I don't have to do it now."

Offering him a small smile, I nod in gratitude. He will give me time, maybe even long enough to hide again. My idea to learn control was stupid. And dangerous. I don't need to mingle with humans to find Roberti. I can do it at night while the majority of them are sleeping. This just proves none of us should be out of those portals. My thoughts must be showing on my face because Leo clears his throat, the corners of his mouth curving down.

"How did you find me anyway?" Tugging the ugly pink t-shirt over my head, I toss it at him. It leaves me in the black tank I had on underneath.

I should've done it sooner.

Turning the monstrosity in his hands, he shrugs and grabs the collar, tearing it wide enough to step through it while wiggling the t-shirt over his hips until it looks like he is wearing a tight, bright pink mini skirt. The horn of the unicorn is poking out like an arrow from his erection. I swear the wolf is horny twenty-four seven. He chuckles when he sees me staring at his groin.

"A legend." He nods, male satisfaction clear as day from

the swaying of his hips and grin on his face. I groan in exasperation.

"You are so humble you put Zoltan to shame."

"I know." His face is so serious that, despite myself and the situation I'm in, I bark out a laugh.

"You still didn't tell me how you found me." I know I need to move away from here but my feet are glued to the floor.

Leo tilts his chin at something ahead, to my right and I lean forward to see what he is pointing at. My heart skips a beat when I see Daren sitting on the hood of a car with his arms crossed over his chest. It has to be the control, which I'm hanging onto by a thread that stops me from noticing either one of them. This is not good news. I can prevent humans from sensing what I am, but it'll leave me open to attacks I'll never see coming.

"I see you are realizing the pros and cons of walking among the humans in the daylight." Leo nods and Daren gets to his feet, sauntering closer to us.

"I just had to find Myst and latch onto her signature." The mage won't look me in the eye. "She's a slippery one, but nothing I can't handle if I put my mind to it." I believe him. The guy waltzed inside the academy like he owned the place.

"Don't tell her that. She might kill you if she knew." Snorting, I look from the alpha to the mage.

None of them think that's funny, but it's probably more because it's actually true. She won't rest until Daren is dead, not if she knows he can track her and find her anytime. My eyes widen at that. "Don't you dare tell her that."

"I find it interesting that you don't trust her, yet you went to her for help, Drake." Leo lifts both hands palms up. "I'm not judging, either. I just find it interesting."

"We have a business arrangement." Pushing off the wall, I stumble slightly before I catch my footing. "The two of you should go. Myst will come looking if I don't go back soon." It's a lie.

They know it, too.

"See, that will be a problem, Drake." Leo falls in step with me, and Daren takes the back. "If I go back, I'll have to lie to Zoltan, right to his face. No one wants that, trust me." All three of us ignore the dead human we are leaving behind.

"Your plan is what exactly? To follow me around until you have to go back?" Yanking the door to the stairway open with more force than necessary, I take the stairs two at a time. Unfortunately, the two males don't disappear in the dust behind my rushed footsteps.

"Something like that." Leo snickers.

We reach the bottom level of the mall where the human male walked up to me. The three of us cross it to the sliding-glass entrance, attracting stares from the humans even while all of us are in control of the effect we have on them. Leo's pink mini skirt might have something to do with it. As much as I hate to admit it, he looks sexy as hell wearing the stupid thing, and that's saying a lot because any other male would look ridiculous in it. The cocky bastard even beams and winks at a couple of human females, making them swoon and giggle like school girls.

"Incorrigible." I grumble under my breath while I shake my head at his antics.

"Legendary, Drake." Grinning wolfishly at me, he wiggles his hips. "Epic, I tell ya."

"You are such an idiot, pup." But I laugh because I just can't help myself around the shifter. Daren snickers behind us, coughing to cover it up. "Is that why Astara likes you so much? Because you are epic?"

Leo stiffens next to me, though he covers it with an exaggerated swagger and a too-bright-to-be-real grin. My eyes narrow on his face until I realize they are herding me towards the place where I saw Myst waiting in her car. When I try to stop, both males move in sync to either side, taking me by the upper arms and practically carrying me to the parking spot. We come from behind so poor Myst doesn't see what's about to hit her.

Leo yanks the back door open, and because Tenebris is staring intently at the sliding-glass doors of the mall, it startles him. Now I see that we exited the place through a different side, but it's too late to argue with the manipulative jerks. The alpha, of course acting like his usual self, tricked me by keeping my attention away from what was in front of me. And Zoltan says I'm cunning. I can't hold a candle to these two, not any day of the week.

Myst jerks from the driver's seat, staring daggers over her shoulder at all three of us. I can't do anything but squeak when Daren lifts me off my feet and sends me head-first inside while he scrambles right on my heels. I either move or he will shove his face in my ass, so I crawl faster on the leather seat. Leo is already opening the door from the other side and climbing in, and once he tucks himself inside, he closes it with a loud clap. With their large bodies in the back of the car, I end up mushed next to Tenebris with the panther almost sitting in my lap, which is a definite test to the endurance of my femurs.

Silence blankets the inside of the vehicle, the air charged with so much hostility its stinging my skin. Not all of it is coming from Myst, however. Tenebris is bristling too, glaring at the two males with his upper lip twitching in a barely-restrained snarl. To calm the situation, I scratch under his shin and his lids lower to half-mast a second before the purring starts.

Leo snorts, the jerk.

Tenebris yanks his head away from my hand so hard he hits the alpha's shoulder, and in reaction, Leo's head smacks the window. All four of them now glare at me, including Daren, who is cradling his ribs. He must've hit the door handle when the panther jostled all of us.

"Stop glaring at me," I snap at all of them. "This was a stupid idea, Myst!" I stab a finger in her face. "I killed a human today." Her eyes widen slightly and her lips part to say whatever it is she wants to say, but I've had enough. "And don't start on these two. I neither invited them, nor do I want them here anymore than you do. They are manipulative assholes. There is nothing I can do about it now."

"I'm not Uber." Her jaw tightens and she turns that cold stare on the two jerks. "You have two seconds for one of you to sit in the front or I'll kick you all outside." With a huff, she turns away clinging to the steering wheel with a white-knuckled grip.

I jump up like the back seat is made of hot embers, scrambling over the center console, kicking someone in the face and another in the chest in the process. Grunts and snarls follow my crawl but I plop in the passenger seat with a satisfied smile plastered on my face. Clicking my seatbelt into place, I twist around and burst out laughing at the three grouchy scowls staring me in the face. Daren has a red patch on his jaw that he's rubbing at with his fingers. I guess it was his face I kicked … And Leo has a dirty footprint matching my sneaker at the center of his chest, though slightly to the right. Tenebris hisses at me, the sound raising the short hairs on the back of my neck. He is still pissed I made him purr in front of the others.

"The three of you are more than welcome to leave if you like," I tell them primly, pulling a Fenrir and staring down my nose at them. "It'll save you the agony of sitting in the back seat together while the females take care of business."

It's like flipping a switch. Leo's smile makes an appearance, a knowing gleam entering his gaze. Lacing his fingers behind his head, he slouches in the back seat and purposely spreads his knees wider to give me a great view of his penis. His grin grows at the unimpressed twist of my mouth.

Daren grinds his teeth, a muscle jumping in his still-red jaw as he turns to stare out the window. He is focused on my face with side-eyed glances, which only makes the situation childish and ridiculous. The panther huffs, shouldering a space for himself between the two front seats and folding his front paws on the center console. He leans his large head on them and pretends to sleep, but his swiveling ear gives away his act.

My body pitches to the side when Myst slams her foot on the gas, flying out of the parking spot in reverse like a Formula One racer. My back hits the seat hard enough to push all the air out of my lungs when she hits the break, and then I lurch forward while dangling in the seatbelt when she squeals out of the mall's parking lot.

"You killed a human how?" Zigzagging between moving vehicles, she turns to look at me and my heart jams itself in my throat. We might be immortal but we can still die if we get crushed in car, or, of course, decapitated.

"Keep your eyes on the road." My voice is thick with panic. When she doesn't comply fast enough, I scream at her." Watch the fucking road, Myst."

She turns to do what I asked, but the look on her face tells me I'll pay for it later. That's good. For that to happen, I have to step out of this damn metal contraption alive. This is why I love bikes. I have full control, and I only have *my* life in my hands. Plus, it's easy for me to jump off it if I have to. I might be banged up, but at least I'll be alive.

"The human." She pushes the words through clenched teeth.

"He tried to rape me, so I killed him." Swallowing the bile in my throat, I explain how I finally got control of the energy luring the humans towards me before the vile male dragged me to the underground parking lot. I told them that it wasn't his first time either, mentioning the yellow elastic band I saw instead of reading his emotions.

"The initiation worked." Myst lifts her gaze in the rearview mirror and I hear Leo grunt in affirmation.

"What's that got to do with me killing the human?"

"Did you stop to consider why you went with him when you could've easily walked away?" Daren is the one who speaks.

I frown at the hands folded in my lap, twisting my fingers and gnawing on the inside of my mouth. "No."

"You sensed the evil in him and allowed him to lead you to a secluded place, right?" This comes from Leo.

"I guess …" Trying to recall exactly why I went with the human is like trying to grasp water in my hand. It keeps slipping through my fingers.

"We have an agreement as part of the Accord with the human government, Drake." Leo straightens from his slouch, leaning over Tenebris to see me better. "Sort of like cleaning out their trash. We have no control over it when we come across those humans. We follow until we can remove the threat to the rest of humanity."

"We have no control of our actions?" A new type of fury churns in my stomach.

"None." Daren sighs.

Myst keeps giving me side-eyed glances while I stare at my fingers as if they'll start talking and tell me how to deal with this clusterfuck. Taking a deep breath, I lean my head on the headrest, closing my eyes, and releasing it slowly.

"My plan was to slit the throats of the old assholes on the Board," I tell my folded hands, blinking to clear the red haze from my vision.

"And now?" Myst's voice is barely above a whisper but all of us hear her clearly.

"Now I'm going to make it a very slow and painful death."

"I really like you, Chicca." And for the first time there is fondness in her softly-spoken words.

Chapter Four

I stare unseeing through the window, focusing on my breathing so I don't start screaming in the car. You'd think I'd be used to curveballs being thrown from left field by now. The horrified face of the human floats at the forefront of my churning thoughts, taunting me, his screams rattling the gray mass in my skull. He was a slime, a stain of humanity that needed removing, but I can't help the guilt eating a hole in my stomach for being his executioner.

I've spent most of my adult life removing those like him from the supernatural world. The difference is *they* were still breathing. Taking a deep breath, I release it slowly through pursed lips to make as little noise as possible. With it comes the realization, which is as clear as the first rays of the sun burning my retinas. I'm not bothered that I killed him. The Fates know I've killed my fair share of people. What disturbs my still-fragile brain is the fact that the human stood no chance against me. And I stood no chance of fighting the compulsion to kill him.

Just like my brother.

All because of the fuckers on the Board.

"Drake?" Leo says my name cautiously, pulling me out of the downward spiral threatening to drown me.

"Leave her be, wolf," Myst barks at him, glaring through the rearview mirror.

"I'm fine." Cutting off the argument that's about to create more noise than I can handle at the moment, I force my lips to tilt up. "You can't expect me to just go along with things when you drop a bomb like that."

"Don't." Leo shudders slightly when I turn to see him over my shoulder. "Just don't force a smile, Drake. My wolf gets itchy for a fight."

"What's with everyone telling me not to smile?" Huffing, I straighten in my seat. "You guys are going to make me not want to ever smile again."

"I love it when you smile, but when you force it, it just doesn't look right." Jerking forward, he stabs a finger at the rearview mirror so Myst sees it. "Like that. See? That's asking for a fight."

Twisting around, I turn to Myst and see a feral smile lifting the corners of her mouth. If I look anything like her, I don't blame Astara or Leo for telling me to cut it out. It's unnerving. Her grin grows the more Leo glares at her, the chocolate color of her eyes turning as black as a bottomless pit. Goosebumps pop out on my arms and the short hairs stand on the back of my neck. The second part of me, the entity sharing my body, perks up and intrigue washes through me. Not anger or an instinct to fight, no. It's more like it's amused that Myst is trying to rile the dragon entity up.

Tenebris snorts in a very human-like manner, his hot breath puffing over the skin on my forearm, which is pressed on the center console. It drags my laser-like focus away from

Myst and to him. I swear the panther rolls his eyes before closing them again. His right ear flicks back and forward a couple of times, too.

"What's really bothering you, Franky?" Daren speaks from behind my seat where I can't see him.

The familiar sound of his voice and him calling me Franky do stupid things to my insides, making me slump in the passenger seat. Many times in my life, when I felt messed up or lost, he would ask the same question while filling a frosted glass with beer. All those times, I would vent and ramble like a broken record, telling him as much as I dared and nothing at all. It made me see things clearly when sharing them with my friend. *Not really a friend now, is he?* The snarky voice in my head makes my teeth grind. Shoving it away as deep as I can, I unclench my jaw. Now is not the time to think of my misguided choices in life, be it about friends or anything else.

"Having no control over what I do or who I kill does not sit well with me," I answer him in a growl, flinching at how snappy it sounds.

"That's always been the issue with you, has it not?" Adopting the usual conversational tone that will make me spill my guts, Daren shuffles in the back seat. His words make me stiffen.

"You know nothing about my issues, so don't pretend otherwise." I sound too defensive even to my own ears.

Undeterred, he grabs the back of my seat in his large hands, jostling me when he pops his head to the side. "It's true. Since I've known you, all you've been fighting to gain is control over your life. Somewhere along the way, you convinced yourself that you have no say in it."

"I had no control when I killed the human." My mouth snaps shut as soon as the words are out, which only confirms his observations. Damn the mage and his fucking philosophies.

"Being a half blood is something you can't change, and it's also something that made our own society shun you," he continues like I haven't spoken. "Having parents that, although present, never showed any parental stability was another. Then Andrius swooped in, dragging you into his world by offering a false sense of control. You ate it up like a starving creature, and you looked away from anything he would do that might take that fragile control away."

The silence in the car is suffocating. My fists are clenched so tight my nails are digging in my palms and hitting bone, which makes them slick with blood. Every word that comes from Daren's mouth is muffled through the whooshing in my ears. I can feel Tenebris's attention burning a hole at the back of my skull. The mage is not finished yet, unfortunately.

"He cornered you by holding the job over your head, and he pushed you further into a spinning torrent by sending you to the academy." Bile is scorching the roof of my mouth and the back of my throat. "Once there, the ground was ripped out from under your feet, first by his betrayal and then by Soren, who tied your life to his, which pulled your second nature to the front. I'm sure they meant well, but I blame Zoltan and Fenrir for leading you further into the rabbit hole by taking you through the portal when you were not ready. You haven't stopped fighting for control, yet at every turn you lose it more and more. The initiation was just the icing on the cake."

"Is there a point to all of this?" Swallowing hard, I rasp out, blinking away the burning at the back of my eyelids.

"You didn't have time to stop and process all this." Daren sighs, jostling me again when he wiggles the back of my seat with his arms. "I hoped that's what you were doing while hiding from everyone. I was obviously wrong."

Incredulous laughter bubbles in my throat, mainly because he sounds grumpy for being wrong. I stifle it down because I know it'll sound hysterical and insane. Everything he said swirls in my mind, my thoughts jumbling together until there is only a high-pitched sound bouncing inside of my skull. Even the entity inside me shrinks away from it, crawling to the furthest recesses of my soul until I can't feel it anymore.

When he puts it like that, it's hard to argue his point. Out of everyone, I can honestly say that Daren knows me the best, even if I barely knew him at all. It's just another thing that proves his observation is spot on. Being so self-centered, doing everything I could to prove I was as good as all the pure bloods can do that to a person. It warped my reality into a never-ending loop of bad decisions. According to the mage, I haven't stopped making them either.

"She doesn't need control." My head snaps to Myst, sending a sharp pain up my neck and through my shoulders. She flicks her gaze to the side mirror before zigzagging through the fast-moving cars sharing the freeway with us. The blares of horns and the screeching of tires follow in our wake. "What she needs is acceptance. Control will come with that."

"I agree," Leo grumbles thoughtfully from behind.

"Look at the three of you. You're like the three wise men." Myst cocks an eyebrow at my wording but ignores me otherwise. "I don't need psychoanalyzing; I need action. I've accepted this shitstorm already, thank you very much."

My back hits the door, the curved-out hand rest digging in my spine. The three males in the backseat grunt too, Tenebris hissing angrily as his jaws snap at the air. Myst tightens her grip on the steering wheel and takes the sharp, unexpected exit, though she says nothing. I just chalk it up to her crazy driving skills, or lack there of.

"I can work on my control when I separate Roberti from his head." Straightening, I force the nails to slide out of the skin of my palms and continue. "Until then, I will hunt him at night. That way, there won't be many humans in the way, and I won't lose my instincts while having to control what I am. Problem solved."

"There is a problem with your plan from the start, Drake." Leo gets my attention by tugging on the pink shirt, which has climbed all the way up to his narrow hips like a wide belt. A grimace pulls on his lips when he lifts his ass and drags the pink monstrosity down. "Andrius is a demigod that walks the day. He is dealing with humans here, so he will be out and about during the daytime. Looking for him at night gives only a small window of opportunity to find him."

"That's my problem, not yours." A gasp escapes me when the car takes another sharp turn, sprawling me over Tenebris's head and onto Myst's lap. "What the ..."

"Hold tight," Myst hisses through her teeth, her expression fierce and her eyes glued to the rearview mirror. "Not today fuckers."

I've said it before and I'll say it again. I hate cars. Myst is flooring the gas pedal, the force pushing my body into the unforgiving leather of my seat. The pressure on my chest is like a mountain preventing me from filling my lungs with oxygen. The growls and hisses from the back seat just add to my frustration when I can't even turn around to see what has pushed Myst into psycho mode. More psycho mode than her usual sunny self, that is.

"What's going on?" I almost bite off my tongue when

33

we swerve to the right, the car fishtailing for a few heart-stopping seconds. "Myst?"

"Hunters," she grinds out, white knuckling the steering wheel.

"What are they planning on doing?" A humorless chuckle that sounds strange to my ears passes my lips. "It's the middle of the day. Every human around will see us fighting."

"I'm not sure they care right now." Daren sounds further away, so I'm guessing he has turned to look through the rear windshield.

Wiggling and flopping around, I manage to turn too, hugging the back of my seat for dear life. Sure as hell, there is a black sedan with sleek lines right on our tail. There is no mistaking the white clothing and face coverings the hunters have on, and my heart thunders in anticipation. Daren lifts his elbow in my line of sight, and on reflex, I jerk my head away from it. Good thing I did because I also have to duck behind the headrest when his fist connects to the rear glass of the car, shattering it in small pieces that fall over the top of the seat and the trunk.

"I will skin you, mage," Myst snarls, but somehow, she keeps her attention on the road. Thank the fates.

"Turn right on the next street." Daren has to shout to be heard over the whistling of wind filling up the inside of the vehicle. Orange and red flames are licking the palm of his hand.

Feeling useless, I clutch the headrest finding it hard to breathe when I see Leo holding onto Tenebris with all he's got. The stupid panther is trying to shake off the alpha so he can jump out of the car. I don't know what possessed me, but in a daze, I watch my hand reach for Tenebris, my fingers snatching his lashing tail. The moment soft fur presses on my palm, I jerk on it as hard as I can. Both Leo and Tenebris stiffen, the wolf gaping at me with wide eyes and the panther baring his sharp teeth, his upper lip quivering above them.

"Let him work." Snapping at both shifters, I jerk my chin at Daren and almost bash my head on the window when we take yet another turn.

Daren says something I don't hear, my spine snapping to attention at Myst's answering snarl. Tires squeal like dying beasts over the concrete, humans slamming on their breaks or hitting parked cars on the side of the road to avoid whatever they think is happening here. In the middle of all this, I can't help thinking that we really will be all over the human television now. This situation is like one of the movies I've watched to kill boredom at home.

"I missed them, damn it. Steady the car," Daren throws over his shoulder as newly-formed fire stretches from his palm.

"You want to drive?" Myst snaps, but she wrestles the steering wheel to prevent anymore jostling. "There are craters in the fucking streets, not holes."

"Just hold for a moment." The mage cocks his hand back, Leo, Tenebris, and I leaning away from the heat of his magic. It's a hard task since Myst is not letting go of the gas pedal, but it's a reaction none of us can control. "Let me know when you can take another turn."

The hunters are gaining ground. I watch horrified when the passenger window opens and the hunter sticks half of his body out of it. The black bulge in his hands curdles the blood in my veins. They've never used guns before. As a matter a fact, none of us use weapons other than blades, magic, and our own bodies.

And bombs. Don't forget the bombs, the inner assholish voice reminds me.

Everything around me slows to a crawl as I fight for air, staring at the barrel pointed at us. No, not at us but at the back wheels of our car. They are going to flip us head over ass in this concrete jungle, pressed on both sides by houses two or three stories tall. This is a suburb where families live, and there is no doubt in my mind the collateral damage will be a few human lives. For some stupid reason, my eyes lock on the hood of the hunter's car, my attention zeroing in on the triangular shield with two axes crossed and a lightning bolt piercing between them.

"Turning in two." Myst pushes the words through clenched teeth.

Daren flings the flame out of the back of the car.

I stop breathing, watching the magic sail through the air right at the car behind us. The hunters are so close that if their vehicle explodes there is no way it'll miss us. They don't slow down or try to avoid it. It looks like they speed up, actually, coming so close I can see the hatred burning in both their soulless gazes. Daren's magic hits the windshield of the hunters' vehicle just as a gunshot sounds through the whistling wind. I watch stunned as the sleek car jumps off the road hood first, lifting in the air like a rising monolith of doom. A white streak flings out of their open window before an explosion blasts, lifting the moving wheels of our car off the street.

The force of the blast propels us in the air too, my body going weightless for a long moment.

I really should've kept my seatbelt on, I think stupidly before Tenebris jumps on me, his heavy body flattening me on the front seat. The last thing I hear is Daren chanting before it all goes dark.

Infuriated

It could've been my imagination for all I know.

Chapter Five

Voices come in and out.

At one point, I'm sure I threaten whoever it is with ripping their throats out if they don't shut up. It works. Drifting in and out of sleep, I dream about hunters and their soulless eyes, thick shadows racing through time and space to get to me. Every time, before any of them reach me, flames burst out of nowhere and engulf everything until only fires surround me on all sides. My whole body is on fire, my skin sizzling and melting off my bones while my screams stay unheard.

Through all that torment, I'm still alive.

"I think you had enough rest, Chicca." With a groan, I turn on my side and pop one eye open to squint at Myst.

"Why are you here?" More importantly, I wonder why she's not being her obnoxious self by yelling from the front door or fighting with Tenebris, but I don't want to get her all worked up by mentioning it. "Where is Tenebris?"

There is no way the panther didn't sneak up in my room after I fell asleep. Both my eyes open when Myst just stands there looming over my bed with an unreadable expression. Something bumps the side of the bed, jostling me enough to fight the covers so I can turn around. When I do, I see Tenebris pacing the length of the bed, stealing glances like he doesn't want to meet my eyes. The remnants of the dream still linger, turning my brain to slush, but they are both so unnerving that I force myself to think.

It all comes back with a clarity I wish it wouldn't. The mall, the human, his stench, and terrified screams rattling my skull. Leo and Daren finding me hunched over in the dark underground parking lot, the hunters. And lastly, the chase around the streets and the massive explosion that sent us hurtling in the air. I jerk upright in bed with the covers pooling around my waist, the fact that I'm naked forgotten in the panic.

"Leo? Daren?" My hair whips across my face when I turn from Myst to Tenebris as if the panther will open his mouth and speak to me.

'They are both fine." Folding her arms across her chest, Myst narrows her eyes slightly at me. "You, on the other hand, were hit or miss for a while."

They are fine. That's the only thing that registers in the one blessed moment before I flop down and tug the covers to my chin. *They are fine. Everyone is fine, Franky. Breathe.* I have to repeat it a few times in my mind until my lungs start functioning properly and it doesn't feel like my stomach is lodged in my throat.

Breathing evenly, I turn my head to the side and track Tenebris's pacing. Now that I'm fully awake, I can see patches of his fur have lost their oily shine, instead the ashen color permeating many of the coarse hairs sticking out every which way. He looks agitated but, although I can see the evidence of the explosion on him, he is otherwise unharmed. That's when the second part of what Myst said registers in my thick skull.

"I feel fine." The words sound harsher than I intend. I'm not sure if I'm upset with the hunters, myself, or with her for taking me to that damn place. "How long was I out?"

"Long enough for me to get bored." Cocking a hip to the side, she taps her foot.

"So, like five minutes." Grinning like a fiend at her glare, I roll out of bed. "Not too long I'd say."

It's a very awkward situation when you find yourself pinned by another female while you are butt naked. The sharp dagger digging into the skin of my neck is another problem that I choose to ignore because all the air is pushed out of my lungs when Myst slams my back to the wall. I see Tenebris coiling up to go for her jugular, so I make sure I smile to discourage him from attacking. Even the panther recoils from the curving of my lips, and I huff in frustration. I'm going to take everyone's advice and just stop forcing smiles.

"You think it's funny you almost died on my watch?" Myst snarls against my neck. She is so much shorter than me that this should be comical. But it's not. Especially when she nicks my skin with her blade.

"I didn't think you cared one way or another." Opting to make light of the situation, I buck my hips slightly to encourage her to move. "I'm not sure Tenebris will be shocked for much longer. I'd move if I were you. We've had enough fighting to last us a month."

"If the kitten moves, I will paint this bedroom with his innards. You think what happened out there is a joke?" My back presses hard to the wall when shadows start pulsing out of her body, blurring the edges of her form.

Tenebris snarls a terrifying sound that raises the hairs on the back of my neck. For the first time since she woke me up, I really look at her face. At the downward tilt of her lips, the strained lines at the corners of her eyes, and her pale cheeks with a few red blotches scattered on them. Myst is scared. The shock of seeing that buckles my knees and I sag, pressing my neck harder on the dagger.

"The hunters attacking was not my fault." Slowly, I lift my hand to stop the panther from attacking because his whole body is trembling from the urge. "I've never stepped foot outside this house without you."

"No." Pushing off me, she stomps a few feet away before whirling around. "It was those two jerks, they were being followed. Daywalkers are always bad news no matter the situation." A muscle ticks in her jaw while I watch her warily. "I never should've let them pick up my trail." The last part she mutters under her breath, but I hear it as if she screams it in my face.

"You let them find me?" Anger bubbles up, erasing the worry from her scared look. "I trusted you." I flinch from the obvious hurt in my snarl.

"I told you not to trust me, so don't look shocked, Chicca." Her chin juts out as if daring me to say something. "The worlds are going to shit and you want to hide and plot a petty revenge. This is a wakeup call. Grow up. Nothing in this shitstorm is about you." Glaring, she waves the dagger at me. "And put some clothes on because the stench is getting close."

Left speechless by the venom in her voice, I woodenly walk to the chair in the corner and snatch pants she must've left there, then stab my legs through them. As soon as my shirt is pulled over my boobs the door opens, Leo peeking his head through it. I guess the stench reference was meant for the wolf, not me. Which makes me glad that I resisted the urge to sniff myself.

"You are up." His gaze travels up and down my body before he shoulders the door wide open and enters the bedroom.

It's a small room, so with all of us inside plus the bed, it's already crowded, and that's not counting Daren, who is looking over the alpha's shoulder from the hallway. Tenebris panting and growling low in his chest just adds to the tension saturating the air. I flick my eyes to Myst, wondering how she knew they were coming.

She huffs. "He smells like a wet dog, so it's hard to miss." Myst scowls at Leo like it's his fault that he was born a shifter.

"Charming as always, Myst." Sarcasm drips like molasses from the alpha's words. He tracks the dagger that twirls between Myst's fingers before disappearing in one of the many hidden pockets of her clothing. The female is a walking arsenal, worse than me when I worked for the Agency.

Speaking of which.

"The hunters were tracking the two of you." My gaze flicks between Leo and Daren, the mage grimacing at the alpha's back. "You didn't notice you had a tail?"

"I didn't pay close attention, no." A line forms between Leo's eyebrows, pulling them low over his eyes.

"What he is trying to say is we got so excited that we picked up your trail that he forgot to check if we were being followed," Daren grumbles from behind him.

"And you were doing what, exactly, that you couldn't keep an eye out while he used his sniffer?" The more Daren talks, the more every word that comes out of his mouth gets on my nerves. I'm still messed up from his psychoanalyzing in the car.

"I was tracking the magical signature." Hurt crosses over his face but I ignore it.

"I need to do another sweep of the perimeter to make sure no one is sneaking up on us while we are sitting ducks here." Myst sashays out of the bedroom, knocking Leo back a couple of steps in the process.

"You're such a bitch," I call after her.

"Bitch is my middle name, Chicca. Get over it," she hollers from the living room, and a moment later, the front door closes with a bang loud enough to rattle the windows.

"That female has anger issues." Daren is looking over his shoulder like he is expecting her to come back and tell him off. I wouldn't put it past her.

"I thought that was me." When he snaps his head my way, I can't help but snort. "Being the female with anger issues, I mean." Spreading my arms wide, I shoo them out of the bedroom, Tenebris slinking behind me. "How long was I out? Myst never answered that question."

"Seventy-two hours." Leo wiggles his hand side to side. "Give or take."

I trip over my own bare feet, catching myself at the last minute with a hand on the wall. "Seventy-two ..." I trail off, gaping at the males. "Why didn't you wake me sooner?"

"You were badly burned, Drake." Leo grabs me by the upper arm and leads me to one of the sofas in the living room, depositing me like I'm about to pass out. I am, but that's beside the point.

"You healed me?" I eye Daren suspiciously. I didn't think he could heal.

"Kind of, yeah." Daren fidgets, and my stomach drops to my feet.

"What do you mean 'kind of?'" Both of them look like children caught with a hand in the cookie jar. "What do you mean 'kind of?'" Two predators that will rain death on anyone daring to keep eye contact longer than a second flinch from my shout.

"We gave you Daren's blood and you healed." Leo wouldn't meet my glare.

"Why in the worlds would you feed me the blood of a mage?" My stomach is churning at the thought of them feeding me blood while I was unconscious. I had no say if I wanted it or not. The more time I spend around these people, the more boundaries they break claiming it's for my own good.

"It's what Fenrir and Zoltan do when you've been hurt before. Why wouldn't we?" The alpha sounds defensive as he squares his shoulders. "You are a half vampire, Drake. It's what you do. You drink blood."

"Thanks, I didn't notice I was a half vampire." When the shifter opens his mouth to call me out on the snark, I shove a hand in his face to silence him. "He is a mage, you asshole. I can barely control this thing inside me, and you pumped me with blood that is full of magic. Great fucking job, Leo."

"It was either him or the two of us." He flings a hand between himself and Tenebris. "Your friend Myst bolted the second I mentioned it. Better to deal with magic than to sprout a tail. If something like that happened, I didn't think you'd let me live it down. You are unpredictable." Scowling, he crosses his arms across his chest trying to intimidate me. Like that shit will work.

I guess I should be grateful that neither of them went running to Zoltan screaming about me being hurt. In all this, at least I have that going for me. The last time I saw the vampire and Fenrir was when I slit my brother's throat in cold blood, which led to my own mother calling me every name under the moon. I don't think a lifetime will give me enough time to come to terms with everything before I have to face them. No, the longer I stay away from them, the better. No one else needs to suffer or die because of me.

"I don't like that look on your face," Daren says softly, squinting at me.

"It's the only face I have so get used to it." Hoping to change the subject, I look at a still-put-out Leo. "And I won't smile anymore if I don't feel like it."

"That's the best decision you've made, Drake." Shuddering, the alpha looks so earnest a chuckle escapes me before I can stop it.

"This is like a bad dream. One I can't wake up from." Scrubbing a hand over my face, I lean back on the sofa and gather my wild hair away from the face. "We should be okay here, right?" Still holding my mane back since I have nothing to tie it with, I turn from the wolf to the mage. "It's been seventy-two hours and no hunters have come sniffing around."

"Not that we've noticed, no." At my frown, Leo rushes to reassure me. "I've been patrolling the neighborhood every couple of hours, Drake." Daren stands from the sofa opposite mine heading for the kitchen, and we both only give him a passing glance. "On foot during the day, shifted after it got dark. No one is around apart from humans."

"What time is it?" I feel that I need to do something to make up for all the time I've lost. Sitting around thinking about things has never been my favorite pastime. I'm prone to overthinking and getting myself in a very dark and gloomy place. Better to keep busy.

"It's eight in the evening. They lost the sun an hour

ago." Daren returns with a plate full of sandwiches. "Eat, apart from blood you haven't had anything." He shoves the plate in my face and my stomach grumbles, the sound no different than when Tenebris gets angry. The shifter in question is laying at my feet, but his head perks up at the smell of the food.

I'm still not over being fed mage blood—as well as everything else to be honest—but I nod my thanks to the mage and snatch the food from his hand. Until I take the first bite, I don't even realize I am starving. Tenebris is eyeing the plate while I devour the food, but at the moment I think I'll fight him if he tries to get anywhere near it. Leo and Daren watch me in fascination while I scarf it down, my cheeks bulging out like a chipmunk. Before you know it, I place the empty plate on the low table and sink into the sofa with a groan, patting my belly.

"Thank you, I really needed that," I tell the mage, and his head bobs up and down in acknowledgment. "What's the plan? I need to move. I can't just sit around here."

As if invited, the rumbling sound of mufflers comes from outside. Leo and Daren exchange a look and the alpha strides to the windows facing the front yard, his legs eating the space in two seconds. The growl of a machine is getting louder, and I realize it's not a car but a motorcycle. Pushing off the sofa to join Leo, I'm left half crouched when Daren snatches a jacket that's been thrown over the back of the sofa and rushes to the shifter. My eyebrows hit my hairline when the mage grabs Leo by the arm, muscling him out the front door. Even Tenebris looks confused when I glance at him.

"See you later, Franky." Daren's words are jumbled as the door closes with the click.

"What the fuck was that?" I ask the panther, and obviously I don't get an answer.

The sound is gone, just like the two idiots that ran outside, and finally my body unclenches from the half crouch. Tentatively, I pad closer to the window freaked out about what I will see there. Did the two males have a date or something? What can get them out of here like their ass is on fire? Tugging on the curtain just enough to peek outside, there is no sign of Leo or Daren. No, this is much worse, and my heart lodges in my throat.

"Zoltan."

Chapter Six

On the street in front of the house there is a black race bike tilted to the side and the vampire has his ass parked on it, his glowing eyes locked on mine across the space. Dressed all in black, his hair disheveled from the wind and his skin appearing silverish from the moon, Zoltan has no right to look so breathtaking. His hands are in the pockets of his pants, one ankle crossed over the other while he sits unmoving like he has all the time in the world. Everything female in me reacts to the vampire while he has me locked in his gaze.

"Oh, this is bad." I breathe the words just as Tenebris nudges me so he can squeeze his head to the window. "This is really fucking bad." I swear the damn panther snickers.

"Don't you dare laugh, you jerk." Hissing, I wrestle him away from the too-revealing glass. "Some good you are if you can't chase him away."

Tenebris jerks his head up and looks at me like I've lost my mind. Maybe I have. All I know right now is that I really, really don't want to see Zoltan. Like not now or in the next ten years, maybe more. Or ever. When it comes to him, I'm all bark and no bite. I know he will drag my ass back to Sienna. Like a child instead of a grown ass female, I sneak up to the window again, unable to stop myself. Glutton for punishment, I'm telling you.

"What in the worlds is he doing?" Tenebris doesn't answer, but he does move to the sofa, jumping on it and making the springs squeal like they are a dying beast. Ignoring the shifter, I peek one eye out of the corner of the window to eye the vampire. "He is not going to stay there all night."

Right? I mean he is Zoltan. The vampire doesn't give a shit about anything or anyone and eventually he will realize I'm not worth all this trouble. *And that's exactly what you want him to do, isn't it?* the inner asshole reminds me. Grinding my teeth, I push the thought away. Listening to Daren pull me apart in the stupid car was enough. I don't need to do it to myself.

"Tenebris, get your ass up and go … go bite him or something." The shifter only snorts, and he doesn't even lift his eyelids. "And when did he start taking an interest in bikes?"

Zoltan is still there like a statue, the only thing letting me know he is flesh and blood is the tilting of his head that makes it look like he is moon bathing. I can't stop the flutter of butterflies in my belly to save my life. Since Zoltan normally doesn't ride a bike—a fact I know all too well—I know exactly what it is. It's bait. It's little hard to pay attention to because of the mouthwatering male lounging on it, but my eyes keep jumping from the machine to the vampire. I want nothing more than to go outside and run my hands over both of them, and that's the problem right there. Then the blood spraying in an arch and my brother's head rolling off the metal bed pop to the front of my mind, making bile rise to the back of my throat.

I've lived through a lot of bad and impossible things in my life, but I don't think I'll live through seeing disgust in Zoltan's eyes. Who in their right mind would want anything to do with someone like me? My mother was not far off when she called me a heartless beast and monster. Pressing my back on the door, I slide down until my butt hits the floor. Curling the knees to my chest, I thump my forehead on them. *There is no way he is going to sit there all night. He will get bored and leave.* Not even I believe my own thoughts.

Deciding to wait him out as the best possible option, I get comfortable on the floor. Folding my legs under me and placing my hands on the knees palms up, I take deep, measured breaths. Peace and calm do not come easy with Zoltan only a couple of yards away, but I will persevere. I've dealt with worse odds. When warmth blossoms in my chest and I feel tenderness trickling through the bond I've done everything to block away, I almost jump out of my skin. Grinding my teeth, I ignore it, as well as Tenebris snorting something that sounds like a chuckle. Instead, I focus on my breathing. The same breath that almost chokes me when the door opens with such force it makes me slide down the floor on my ass.

"I've had enough of this shit." Myst marches to where I'm gaping at her from the floor and snatches me by the arm. "You are coming with me."

Stupidly, I let her lift me until my bare feet touch the cold concrete outside the door. "What are you, some psychotic matchmaker?" Struggling to free my arm, she keeps dragging me closer to Zoltan. Adrenaline rushes through my veins and I don't dare glance at him.

"No. Unlike you, I'm actually smart." She doesn't even

bother looking at me. The female is stronger than she looks, I know that much.

"I'm smart." I have no idea why I play along with this idiotic conversation, and the vampire is getting closer no matter how much I dig my heels in.

"You are." My head jerks to the side when she agrees with me. "You are also like that cow who gives milk but keeps kicking the bucket. I don't blame you, you had no one and lived an isolated life thanks to that fucker Roberti. Now is the time to snap out of it." Depositing me in front of Zoltan, she offers him a nod and sprints inside, closing and locking the door.

The click of the lock is like a bullet sinking in my brain.

"Did she just call me a cow?" I blurt out stupidly while staring at Zoltan with wide eyes.

"I believe it was a metaphor." My breath gets stuck in my throat at the intense expression on his face. His deep voice thrums through me like bass, popping goosebumps all over my arms. "Hello, Francesca." That hawk-like gaze doesn't miss the fact that I shiver when he says my name. That damn accent does me in every time.

"Why are you here?" Lifting my chin, I fist my hands so I don't fidget.

One side of his mouth kicks up to show a hint of a fang.

My heart trips on itself, stuttering for long moments before hammering my chest.

"For you." He flicks his gaze across mine like he is looking for something. "I thought it was obvious." His nostrils flare, anger flashing for a second in those blue orbs. I bet he smelled Daren's blood in me, but thankfully he doesn't say a word.

I can act dumb, too.

"Yay!" I even pump my fist in a fake cheer. "You found

me. Congratulations. You can go back now." Spinning on my heel, I manage only to raise my foot off the ground.

A muscular arm snakes around my waist, yanking me against a firm, scorching hot chest. I don't remember Zoltan ever being this warm. "I don't think so, love." His breath tickles the skin on my neck before he buries his face there.

"Did it occur to you that I'm here because I didn't want to be found?" My heartbeat is in my throat, which makes my words come out breathless.

"Yes."

"Yes? That's it?" Wiggling like an eel, I turn in his arms and come face to face with him. Bad fucking idea. "I'm not going back there." It takes a lot of effort to not allow my eyes to drop to his lips. My body is shaking from it.

"You fear me." Misinterpreting my reaction, Zoltan spears his fingers in my hair and yanks my face up so he can see me better. "You, out of everyone, should never fear me."

"I'm not afraid of you." My treacherous body melts, molding to his chest as he tightens his hold. "You should be scared of me." Voicing the one thing I refuse to acknowledge this whole time, I fight the tears burning at the back of my eyes.

"Is that so?" The familiar trademark smirk makes an appearance.

"You saw what happened at the academy." Swallowing the bile that threatens to come up, I force myself not to look away from his confused face. "I killed a human, too."

"What were you doing with a human, love?" The possessive way his voice deepens and the blue of his eyes is darkening make my pulse speed up.

"You totally missed the point of what I'm saying." It takes a couple of pushes for him to release me, but it allows me to move away from him and the hold his nearness has on my whole being. "You were captured, turned feral, and you're dealing with all this shit because of me. I also killed my own brother, and now a human for no particular reason. I'm bad news, so you should stay away from me."

"That's for me to decide." Reaching up, he takes my hand and tugs me closer again without manhandling me, which I appreciate. "I think we went over my capture. Everything that happened would've happened with or without your input in it. That's not the reason you hid from me."

"No." I owe him that much at least. "I couldn't face any of you after … my brother." I hate the burning in my eyes and I hope I don't start crying in front of him.

"And what were you planning to do after you hide?" The tight lines at the corners of his full mouth soften while he makes tiny circles with his thumb on the back of my hand. "After coming here?"

"I'm going to kill them, Zoltan." Keeping my focus on his gaze, I make sure he understands that I'm serious about this. "The Board and Roberti made me a killer. I'll show them what they created. I just need to come to terms with it in my own messed up head."

"Okay."

"Okay?" Taken aback, I blink at him. "I really hate it when you talk with one word sentences."

"I know." At my glare, he chuckles, and the sound weakens my knees. "In all this, Francesca, you keep forgetting one fundamental fact."

Frowning, I stay quiet because I have no idea what he is talking about. If he says the Board can't be killed, I'm going to lose my shit right here. Even if they can't, I'm going to spend a few hours a day slicing them up so they can put themselves together for the next day. Nothing will convince me otherwise.

"You forget that I'm on your side." My heart stops when he gives me a genuine smile at the shocked look I know is plastered over my face. "We are a team, you and I, Francesca Drake. Even when you do your best to push me away." My face burns from mortification remembering all the stupid words I threw in his face in Daren's house. What an idiot I am. "Your enemy is my enemy, and I don't take it lightly when someone tries to harm what I consider mine."

"That's the worst caveman line I've ever heard," I snap at him, but my feet shuffle closer to his body. "I didn't want any of you looking at me like I was a monster after what I did." Taking a deep breath, I blow it out slowly. "My plan was to kill them then let the four of you decide my fate."

"The four of us?" Zoltan tucks stray hairs behind my ear, his hand lingering on my face.

"You, Fenrir, Astara, and Leo." My eyes close when he guides me in the circle of his arms, pressing my head to his chest. I can hear his heart thundering under my cheek. "No one else has earned the right to decide if I should live or die. "

"I like that." The deep tones of his voice rumble under my ear.

"Of course you do." Chuckling uneasily, I tilt my face up to look at him. "I'm serious."

"I know you are, but the only fate we will decide is how to remove the threat. If anyone wants to get to you, they'll need to go through me. I'm very certain the others feel the same." Cupping my face, his skin rasps over my cheekbone. "Know this… I will have to be dead for anyone to get to you, Francesca."

"I'm not worried that they'll get to me." I never really

cared about dying now that I think about it. Not that I want to die or something, but if I have a goal, that's what always matters most. The thought of survival is always fleeting, if that. "I don't have a death wish, but I'm worried they'll get to me before I get to them."

"So, what are you doing here?" I don't answer him for a long moment because it's hard not to get lost in his gaze, especially when his entire focus is on me.

"I was practicing shielding myself so I can find and kill Roberti." Omitting that I'm not sure I can bring myself to kill the old farts is a good thing. Thank fuck my brain is still working, though I will admit I sound way too dreamy, almost like a schoolgirl with a crush.

"Okay." Zoltan nods thoughtfully. "And you only want to kill the Board because of what happened with your brother?"

"Isn't that enough?" He opens his mouth, but I wave him off. "I know what you mean. I just had to say it. I think they are working with Roberti. One, two, or maybe even all three of them, but at this point I don't care." When one of his eyebrows arches up, I huff at him. "Soren either knows and doesn't care, or doesn't know and doesn't care. Out of all of them, the Fae is the only one I'm planning to ask. The rest will die the first chance I get."

"Very well. I'll ask again, then. What are you doing here?" My lips part but he presses a finger on them to shut me up. "What better way to get them than to be around them and learn their weaknesses? I normally stayed away from the Board because I never could stand the power-hungry plotting and manipulations. They will have my full attention now."

"I don't think I can be in their presence without

attacking them. This is not a good idea." My head bounces on his chest when he laughs.

"I wouldn't expect anything else from you, and neither would they." Lifting off the bike, he takes me with him toward the front door, tucking me under his arm. "You just be you, and leave the rest to me."

"Where do you think you are going?" I protest, but my feet are moving alongside his on their own.

"To get whatever things you have here. I'm looking forward to riding that bike with you on it." He smirks when a shiver rakes my spine.

"And we are going where?" I know I sound like a dumbass but I can't believe what's happening. How did he just pop up out of nowhere and change all my plans?

"Back home." Is his simple answer.

Home. The word sends longing and rage through my veins.

This is going to be another clusterfuck.

Chapter Seven

Out of all thoughts that should be swirling through my head when I step foot through the portal, the fact they were right about it getting easier the more you use it should not be one of them. I can't help feeling relieved I'm not on my knees emptying the contents of my stomach, though. A pathetic little flutter bursts in my chest when the beauty of my world greets me, the pregnant moon bathing it in silver light from her low perch in the sky. I have no idea why I'm nervous like an idiot. My entire life so far was spent here, yet I'm debating on spinning on my heel and bolting back to the human realm.

I have a feeling Zoltan, Leo, Tenebris, and Daren know this because they have me mushed between them as if I'll try to escape. It's only fitting to be brought here like this, surrounded by dangerous males like some deranged killer. My feet still want to turn and take me away from this place, although I'm calmly closing the space all the way to the tall front doors of the academy.

You shouldn't fear facing them. They should cower before you. My blood turns to ice at the purring voice in my head, but the alpha breaks through my panic.

"I need to check on my pack." Leo looks apologetic but I can tell he is itching to get away from the tension radiating off me. "Daren, you can come along if you wish. We will find them after."

The mage gives me an assessing glance, absentmindedly rubbing the black ink on the back of his hand. "Sounds good. I have no desire to come across anyone in this place." Anyone meaning his father, who we haven't had a chance to discuss.

My lips part so I can say exactly that, if only to push away the still lingering feeling of dread, but Zoltan takes me by the upper arm and onehandedly yanks the heavy double doors open. Steering me straight for the hallways that will lead us to our rooms, he grunts something affirmative, Tenebris following his example by puffing out harsh air through his mouth. The panther is walking so close to me I feel his hot breath on my hand. Somewhere between the first time I saw the shifter until now, he has become someone that centers me in reality when the ground starts shifting under my feet. My fingers sink into his fur and he presses closer still, his shoulder bumping my hip.

"I've been thinking ..." Zoltan manages to irk me without even turning my way. I give him a side-eyed glance and, sure enough, one of his eyebrows is cocked up at my words.

"You've been thinking?" he prods, but I lose my train of thought when my skin prickles from all the eyes turned our way.

The vampire may not notice, but I see everyone giving us a wide berth and avoiding eye contact with me. They must've heard what happened at the disaster of an initiation

I had. I never cared one way or another what anyone thought of me, but sure as all hells the energy coming off them doesn't sit well with me. My fingers tighten in Tenebris's fur.

"Francesca?" I'm sure saying my name was meant as a question, but Zoltan purrs it deep in his chest sending shivers through me.

"Did you have time to look through the book?" The familiar surroundings of the sconces flickering down the hallway scattered on the gray walls unknots the stiff muscles in my shoulders. "Do we have an inkling why they wanted to get their hands on it, apart from the obvious of course?" It's bold to be talking about it in the open when even the walls have ears, as Argoz would like to say.

The quality in the air changes like a switch being flipped. All scents of the different types of creatures roaming the building are erased, replaced by a crisp, cold breath searing my lungs. Like that moment just before a storm hits the shore, the particles are charged with electricity and it lifts the fine hairs on my arms, making all my instincts come to life. I can't see it, but I feel it crackling around me, and I almost look up expecting lightning to strike from the roof.

Zoltan's feet slow and he nudges me behind his shoulder, placing himself between me and whatever—or whoever— is coming our way from around the corner. Tenebris crouches low to the ground, his eyes glowing faintly in the dimly-lit hallway. The first thing I notice when the person comes into view is the ugly scar on the side of his face. It was too much to hope that I wouldn't see Silas, or in this case his son the moment I came back here.

"Zoltan, I was looking for you." The much younger

vampire flicks his cold eyes my way, a muscle twitching on his upper lip before he can take control of it.

"You found me." My one-word wonder sounds casual, but his power is barely contained, which I know because it prickles my skin. Sidestepping me, he cuts the other male's view of me. "What can I do for you?"

"Father said you need to feed." I peek over Zoltan's shoulder when I hear that, confusion spurring my curiosity that the jerk will offer his blood. That's when I notice the girl standing behind the pureblood, her eyes demurely lowered to her feet. "He said you know the rules."

There is white noise inside my head.

Zoltan moves but not even he is fast enough. There is a black blur streaking in front of me, and when the red haze clears, I have Silas's son on the wall by his neck, his feet kicking at least a foot off the floor. My whole body is pressed to his as I hold him there, my magic sending pulse after hard pulse and feeding off his fear. Where my skin touches his, revulsion and hatred for me shoots from him, coating my senses like slime.

"Maybe I need to feed, too." Snarling in his face, I love when his skin pales more than usual. "What do you say, pure blood? You seem very accommodating."

Tenebris rumbles deep in his chest, the sound terrifying enough that I turn to look at him over my shoulder. He has Zoltan pinned on the opposite side holding him back, and the girl is crumpled on the ground blood pooling under her from the four gashes opened on her torso. The panther is as tall as Zoltan when standing on his hind legs, his body a killing machine made of pure muscle that's bunching with each flick of his tail.

"Control your creature, Zoltan." Silas's son sounds

choked up, but he can't help but be an asshole. "Father will not be pleased when he hears of this."

"Make sure you tell him straight away." I give him my craziest smile. "He can come see me so we discuss the issues he has with me." Tilting my head to the side, I can't pinpoint what it is about him that seems off. "Or I can just kill you now and go tell him myself."

"Let him go, Francesca." Zoltan doesn't seem at all concerned that Tenebris has his sharp teeth an inch from his face. "They are just fishing for information the only way they know how. Silas is as diplomatic as a bull in a china shop."

"I'm sure no one will miss him if he is dead." I keep eye contact with the vamp, my grin growing when the jerk hisses profanities at me.

I let him see my pupils change from their usual form to the vertical ones of my Dragon Blood, his face changing with it, the tiny veins under his pale skin fluttering like butterflies. The scar on his face is more detailed like this, and for the first time I notice what looks like a large tooth mark right at the edge of the puckered skin. He redoubles his efforts to push me away when he sees me staring at it in fascination.

"Whatever tried to kill you, it's unfortunate it didn't succeed," I whisper, and his body shudders.

I haven't forgotten his involvement in the ambush the Board created not long ago. Him and his lackeys were all too happy to hurt innocent people for coming to help us save Zoltan from Roberti's clutches. The more I think about it, the less I feel inclined to release him. The clearing of a throat pulls me back from the debate I'm having about whether or not I should just kill the sucker now and be done with it.

"I knew you were back." Fenrir sounds too cheerful for the situation I created in this hallway. "It was way too quiet without you." He chuckles as if we are sharing jokes.

"You are not helping," Zoltan mumbles, but his lips are tilted at the corners when I glance at him.

The Fae is using the wall for support, leaning on it, his gaze betraying the lie of his nonchalance when it scans me from head to toe searching and assessing. Those illusion-created blue eyes are too sharp and the set of his shoulders too stiff to pull it off. *Or you know him too well and you notice those things,* I tell myself.

"Good to see you, Hellion." A blinding smile appears on his perfect face and he winks. "I would've thought my mind was playing tricks on me if I didn't find you like this." His hand flicks at the vampire I still have pinned to the wall.

Tenebris backs away from Zoltan and allows him to straighten his shirt, but none of them move my way. I can feel my eyes shifting as my sight changes to brighter colors flickering in short pulses. Struggling with it, I wrestle control back and shove away from the bloodsucker.

"Get out of my face," I bark at him, and he tosses the girl over his shoulder, disappearing like a cockroach around the bend.

Zoltan walks up to me and tugs me close to his body. When his arm circles my shoulders, I stiffen slightly, but if he notices he doesn't show it. This side of him where he is patient and gentle is far from who I know him to be. It's arresting and it throws me off guard. I bet that's his intention too, because he can't hide that arrogant smirk.

"It appears you were right, Zoltan." Fenrir pushes off the wall and folds his hands in the pockets of his pants. "She didn't fight you too much about coming back."

The truth of his words is like a slap in the face. For all

my talk and attitude, I did tuck tail and come back like a fool without too much convincing. With every intention to punch the Fae in the mouth for daring to point it out, I squirm out of Zoltan's hold but only manage one step. The hallway spins like a vortex, and before I know it, the floor is raising to meet my face. Two sets of arms grab me, preventing me from diving face first into the pool of blood the girl left behind. The stench coming out of it overpowers rational thought and I gasp for air, clawing at their fingers to release me.

"What is wrong with her." Fenrir sounds panicked, his words muffled from the spinning happening inside my head.

"Francesca, breathe." Zoltan's lips are brushing the skin on my ear, his breath hot on my face. "What ..." he trails off when I franticly point at the blood painting the ground.

Zoltan leads me away from it and I see through my tear-filled eyes the blurry outline of Fenrir's body crouching over the stain. Those few steps make a big difference, the clear air sewing through my nostrils as I pant while clinging to Zoltan's arms. The Fae jumps up, taking a few steps away from it too.

"What in the fates is this?" Skirting around it as if it will bite him, he joins us. "I had to get close to smell it but there is something not right with her blood."

"You don't say." I gasp, fighting the dizziness. "I have no idea how I missed the stench until now."

There is an exchange of hands that hold me up and Zoltan cautiously approaches the blood on the floor, his nostrils flaring. He doesn't get too far before jerking to a stop, a feral growl vibrating his chest. Tenebris, on the other hand, is staring intently at it, the only movement coming from the tip of his tail lazily curling in half circles.

"It doesn't seem to bother him." At Fenrir's confused

expression, I point my chin at the panther. "He is much closer than I was."

"It wouldn't." Zoltan turns to face us, murder written all over his handsome face.

"What do you mean?" The hallway stops spinning and I bat Fenrir's hands away now that I can stand on my own two feet. Darting a glance at the blood, my stomach churns when the flickering flames of the sconces happily reflect on it.

"Neither you or I noticed it before because it's a slow working poison. She must've ingested it before being brought here." Zoltan rolls his head around, a muscle jumping in his jaw. "It doesn't bother Tenebris because it's not meant to harm him. It'll harm a vampire, but nothing else."

"I should've killed that weasel." A vicious cry of the panther follows my snarl.

"I think you've done enough killing." The smile on Zoltan's face is not pleasant at all. Tremors rake my spine at the sight. "This one was meant for me. I will deal with it."

"I have a feeling there is a story here." Fenrir perks up as if talking about killing is his favorite pastime. "Let us get out of the open. I can't wait to hear more about it."

"The question is, did Silas send his son here"—I allow them to steer me around the pool of blood, holding my breath so we can get out of this damn hallway— "or did he do it on his own."

"Does it matter?" Zoltan takes my hand as soon as we clear the drying patch on the floor.

"Of course it matters." I give him a look like he is out of his mind. "It's just more proof that the Board is working with Roberti and trying to pick us off one by one."

"The hunch you feel is good enough, Francesca."

My head snaps to the side at his words and I gape at him. *He'll just take my word for it?* all my thoughts screech to a halt. No one has ever just taken my word for anything, little less something as fundamental as this. I'm not sure if I should feel happy, start crying, or what. My entire life I've had to prove everything.

"Just like that?" I can't help but ask, Fenrir already nodding his head in agreement as a loose strand of platinum hair falls over his eye.

"Just like that." Zoltan's lips twitch at the corners.

"Now what?" The hammering in my chest slows down when a familiar set of doors come into view.

"Now we make a plan, and then we hunt." Goosebumps pop out all over my arms at the promise of death in Zoltan's words.

Chapter Eight

It's crazy how you get comfortable around inanimate objects, unimportant things that make you take a step back and release that weary sigh you didn't even know you needed to get out. Leaning my back on the headboard, my body molds to the mattress supporting my weight, all the tension draining from it and leaving me zoned out in a puddle of boneless goo. After having a quick shower and changing into clean clothing, I can't lift my eyelids more than halfway to save my life. Zoltan and Fenrir left in search of that weasel, and hopefully by now they are beating the truth out of him about the poisoned blood. Though they left me with the panther who won't leave my side for anything.

"What is it with these jerks and their poison?" Murmuring under my breath, I jab my toe into Tenebris's ribs.

My heart punches the roof of my mouth when he snaps his jaws a hairsbreadth away from my foot, those emerald eyes glittering with a dare to try and do that again.

Stretched out perpendicular to me, he occupies a lot of space on the bed, personal boundaries an unknows concept to him.

"You're not helping." Grumbling at his assholish attitude, my eyes dart around the room, not snagging on anything for longer than a split second.

Thoughts that I've pushed aside since the initiation assault me, barreling through my head with a vengeance. I doubt the disgust I have for myself will ever go away, but now that some time has passed and somewhat rational thoughts can pierce the humming of fury and rage churning inside me, I can't stop myself from analyzing this whole clusterfuck. Unable to bring a particular one to the front of my mind, I give Tenebris a flicking glance. The shifter has been a pain in my ass since the night I saw him perched on the thick branch of a tree in the forest. Time to make him regret his decision to attach himself to me like a freaking leech I simply can't get rid of.

"We know that Roberti is trying to wake a Titan and bring down the portals so we have war with the humans again. It fits his profile perfectly to want to be at the top of the power pole. He is a demigod of war after all, so it's in his genes to crave blood." One of those emerald eyes peeks from a half-open eyelid, Tenebris either debating where I'm going with this or if he should rip my throat out to shut me up.

You never know with felines, the assholes they are.

"Using the grudge the rest of the species harbored against the vampires for centuries, he managed to recruit a good number of them to infiltrate this place. He had eyes and ears inside the academy even when he was roaming the human world, spreading his operation and working on his plan." My eyes narrow to slits when Tenebris swivels his ear like a damn satellite.

At least he is paying attention.

"What I've come to understand is he wanted me out of the picture so he sent me here." The panther's upper lip curls over his sharp teeth. I'm not sure if he thinks I'm stupid for pointing out the obvious, or if he is pissed because it's a fact. "That's until he realized I'm not just your typical half blood. That night when Soren created the blood bond changed everything, not just for Roberti but for all of us." Tenebris is fully alert now, intently watching me with both eyes open.

A thrill goes through me, all the drowsiness I felt after the shower forgotten.

"We twerked his plans and, so far, all we've been doing is running around fighting left and right with no clear goal in mind apart from killing the fucker." My upper body lifts off the bed, my blood pumping faster with each word coming out of my mouth. "Or that's what he wanted us to believe. I know that jerk and he always has a backup plan for his backup plans. We are getting sidetracked by getting rid of his expendable fighters while he is building a hybrid-mutated army in the human realm."

The thought of my brother slams inside me like a sledgehammer, my eyes losing focus when the memory of his head rolling off the metal hospital bed shrivels my heart. I never knew he existed, and I'll never have the chance to know him. *Because you killed him, you monster,* a voice just like my mother's snarls in my head.

Blinking furiously, I push it away, swallowing the bile burning my throat.

"We are missing something here." Even Tenebris has his head up, my adrenaline rush rubbing off on him. "Roberti keeps sending one minion after another to keep us busy. We are chasing our tails while he is working on executing his plans. I know I'm right on this." Stabbing a finger in the panther's face, I can feel my heartbeat in my mouth. "They are coming at us from all sides. It's like they are a fucking octopus or something. They have just enough weight in their attacks to make us think they planned it, but in reality, they simply get us out of his way."

My breath is sawing out of my lungs, too loud in the silent room.

"What are we missing?" My gaze flicks across Tenebris's emerald eyes. "What is it he doesn't want us to see? I know I somehow played into his hand. I act first, think later. He used that against me, and I dragged everyone else along for the ride too. I'm rash, and Roberti knows that better than anyone else."

Tenebris lifts off the bed, gracefully jumping off it and stopping at the closed door. I'm not sure if he thinks I've lost my mind or he is agreeing with me. His entire body is coiled up, and a low, feral sound is coming from his chest. *'Oh! He agrees and wants me to get my ass up to do something about it.'* I stare at him wide eyed knowing I need to move, but to do what exactly? What am I missing?

The panther releases a roar that rattles the windows, his shoulder hitting the wooden door so hard I'm surprised it doesn't rip it off the hinges. Urgency makes me jump off the bed, but all I do is stand in the middle of the room, panting. *Think! Think! Think!* I shout in my head.

"They know we have the book." My blood curdles and I sway on my feet. "They were searching for the book while I was being stupid in the human realm."

It's me that almost rips the door off the hinges when I yank it open with so much force it bangs loudly off the opposite wall. Dashing out of my bedroom, my feet barely touch the ground.

I have to find Zoltan.

It occurs to me that I can just go into his room and find the book, but it is a fortress all on its own. There is no doubt I'll search until I pass out and I still won't find it. That thought slows the frantic hammering in my chest just enough that I don't hyperventilate.

"He is smart enough to expect someone to be looking for it." Huffing the words, I take the corner a little too fast, my hands hitting the wall the only thing preventing me from knocking myself out.

Tenebris streaks pass me, his feline form loops down the hallway is a thing of beauty to watch.

Pushing aside all the panic, I concentrate on the bond I have with the vampire, latching onto it with everything in me. The entity sharing my body perks up lazily, the warmth of the magic spreading through my limbs. Soft rainbow colors come alive all around me, threads of life revealing themselves in front of my eyes. Through it all, a bright cord as thick as my forearm guides my feet through the building, passing arched entryways and massive peeked windows. The magical flames of the sconces flicker like stars in my peripheral vision, my hair fanning behind me like a surrendering flag. I keep my eyes on the disappearing form of Tenebris, the panther faster than even I can move.

I ignore the stares from those lingering outside of their rooms, though their eyes follow me as I run as fast as my legs will carry me, like the barrel of a gun pointed at the back of my head. The disturbing fact is they don't even bother showing any type of reaction to my mad dash. As if they see people running around here every day.

Or they've seen you do it enough times that they know you are a fruit loop. The sarcastic voice in my head makes me frown.

The thud in my chest when I pass the golden hallway leading to Soren's rooms is sharper than usual but I don't have time to dissect what it means. Pretending not to see the dining hall entrance, I near the offices we used as our base of operations before Zoltan was taken. I should've known I'd find him here. Too focused on the door where I feel Zoltan's presence, I miss the movement coming from my right. A body slams into my side, taking me down with it. We roll on the floor until the body hits a wall, cushioning my impact and elbowing me in the boob in the process.

On instinct, I wrap my arms around one large bicep and, twisting my hips, flip the asshole over until I'm straddling his wide chest. Grabbing whoever it is by the neck with one hand, my other arm cocks above my head ready to pulverize his face. The curtain of my loose hair prevents me from seeing the stupid idiot who thinks he can take me down so easily.

"If you want to jump me, Drake, all you have to do is ask nicely." Leo wheezes, unable to breathe from the tight hold I have on his neck, but his voice freezes my raised fist. "I always did peg you as a girl who likes being on top."

My muscles unclench and I drop my ass hard on his stomach, which makes him grunt and tighten his abs. The alpha is built out of rock, not flesh and bone. It's like sitting on a brick wall. "What the fuck is the matter with you." Angrily swatting the hair out of my face, I glare at him. "Who attacks someone out of nowhere for fun?"

"In my defense"—Folding his hands behind his head, Leo gives me a crooked grin— "I thought someone was chasing you. By the time I realized you were running on your own, I couldn't stop the momentum. I was only trying to protect you."

"How nice of you to protect the poor, defenseless girl." Snarling, I shove off him, making him grunt again.

"A guy can't catch a break around you, Drake." Jumping to his feet, he smooths his hair, which is sticking out all over the place. "Do you blame me for thinking you had a horde chasing you?"

"If there was a horde, do you really think I'd be running?" Insulted by his assholish comment, I tug none too gently on my shirt because it has crawled all the way up to my boobs in our tussle.

"Actually, you are stupid enough to face whatever it is alone." His eyebrows dip over his green eyes like this is the first time something like this has dawned on him and it's unsettling him.

"Stupid?" If looks could kill, the alpha would be dead by now.

"Brave." Both his hands shoot up in the air, palms up. "I meant brave." My mouth opens so I can rip him a new one, but his next words make me forget what I am about to say. "Why were you running, Drake?"

"Oh shit. I have to find Zoltan." I'm already moving again, and the alpha is right on my heels. "It's good that you are here."

Tenebris is pacing in front of a closed door, his lips curled into a snarl. Saliva is dripping from his jaws, and the deep emerald of his gaze looks like it's burning from the reflections of the flames. Leo's wolf reacts, the growl vibrating his chest right behind me in answer to the agitated panther. At least they both stay out of my way when I barrel through the door in a rush.

One second, I'm yanking the door open and stepping

through to get the vampire. The next, my back is slammed on the wall, two sharp fangs grazing the skin on my neck. Hot air puffs out, skirting my throat and raising goosebumps all over my arms.

"Either kill me or get off me, jackass." Zoltan lifts his head until the tips of our noses almost touch. "Well?" My eyebrows crawl up my forehead when those piercing blue eyes don't even blink.

"You smell of fear." Zoltan's deep voice resonates inside my chest where we are pressed close together.

"The book." My heart picks up again. "I think all these attacks are just to keep us distracted while they search for the book."

Zoltan doesn't bat an eye, though he is still searching my face with his nostrils flaring. "You also smell like a shifter." His head turns slowly to the left, the glow in his gaze intensifying.

"Hey, she was running. I thought she was being chased." Leo takes a step back before catching himself. The alpha in him rears its head, making him scowl at both of us. "You can't tell me you wouldn't think she was about to get killed if you saw her sprinting through the hallways!"

"Seriously?" Gaping incredulously at the asshole mutt, I'm being ignored by the two males. "You two can pull your dicks out and measure them later." Snapping at both of them, I shove Zoltan away. Well, I try to shove him away anyway. He is an unmovable rock.

Dumb as one, too.

"Did you hear what I said?" When I wiggle so he can release me, his body leans harder on mine, his erection poking me in the lower belly and impossible to miss.

"No one will find the book." There is an undertone to his voice that I've never heard before, and it stops my attempt to move. "Stay still." The vampire buries his face in my neck, his nose pressing hard on my skin. His lungs fill with deep breaths as he breathes me in.

I almost laugh when I turn to see Leo's shocked face. His eyes are about to pop out of their sockets, his jaw hanging loose. I don't laugh because I yelp when Zoltan's hands tighten on my upper arms, his fingers making the bones almost crack. He jerks back at the pained sound, the color draining from his face.

"I hurt you." Zoltan takes a step back and I stupidly miss the feel of his body on mine.

"That's a joke compared to what will happen if they get the book." I know I'm like a mule who is repeatedly saying the word book, but I can't help it. I have a horrible feeling that I'm right and we are too late.

Leo doesn't make a sound, and neither does Tenebris, who is standing in the middle of the room glaring at all of us. Zoltan keeps clenching and unclenching his fists for a while before his shoulders finally stop bunching up. "I will show you if it'll give you peace of mind," he tells me.

A small smile curls my lips, the fact that he is willing to check making me lean on the wall harder so I don't drop on my ass. Too late, I look around the room, the same space I thought was empty until this very moment. Fenrir, Astara, Argoz, and Daren watch me like they've never seen me before. With a frown I scan the rest of the room. The air punches out of my lungs when my eyes connect with my mother's.

"Hello Francesca."

Chapter Nine

"You can't avoid her forever." Fenrir makes an effort to keep up with me. I'm practically running down the halls, you'd think I'll go hide in my room. Okay, fine. I *am* running to my room.

Fuck the book, and fuck Roberti.

"Listen to me, Francesca." The Fae keeps going like an annoying mosquito buzzing in my ear. "We explained to Sophia how the initiation works. She doesn't blame you for what happened."

"How dare you!" Whirling on him, he stumbles back when I shove with all I've got against his shoulders. "What is it with you people and the inability to stay out of my life? I didn't ask any of you to talk to her or justify my actions. Initiation or not, the fact remains the same. I killed my brother." I hate that my voice breaks as my fists pound on Fenrir's chest with each word. "I did it. I killed him."

"Fenrir, if you may." Zoltan pulls me away from the Fae, his touch gentle despite my flailing around. I didn't even see him follow us out of the room.

"I'll find the two of you later." With one last long, searching look, Fenrir turns on his heel and walks away.

I watch his retreating back, dreading the conversation I know is coming. Just because I listened to Zoltan and came back to this stupid place without a fight doesn't mean I'm over things. As a matter a fact, I'm not over anything really. I'm just a pro at deflecting anything that has the ability to cripple me, mentally and emotionally.

You are as screwed up in your head as ever'. Unfortunately, I agree with the voice in my head on this one.

"I believe you wanted to see that the book is safe." I give Zoltan a darting glance, keeping my head straight while still staring down the now-empty hallway.

"I don't want to talk about it." The grinding of my teeth is too loud in my ears.

"I'm not asking you." His strong fingers curl around mine and he tugs on my hand, wordlessly asking me to move.

With a sigh, I let him turn me around and guide me to his room. "You seem to be back to your old self," I blurt out because I'm unable to handle the silence.

"You do have a talent to push me to the limit of my control and bring me back to sanity with just a look, Love." When he notices I'm staring at his profile, Zoltan doesn't look back at me, but that smirk on his lips makes my palms itch to slap it away. "It is a gift."

"Jerk," I mumble, and he chuckles.

"One that you will have to deal with for a very long time." His hold on my hand tightens and his thick fingers lace through mine. "I do not understand why you're still fighting it."

"You think you are irresistible? How very humble of you Daywalker." Frowning, I glance over my shoulder when understanding hits me about why everything feels so strange. "Where did Tenebris go?"

"He didn't follow you." At my confusion, he offers an arrogant grin. "It takes a brave male to come after you when you have murder written all over your face, Love. One might say I have a death wish."

"Fenrir followed too," I point out like I'm stabbing a needle into his ballooning ego.

"I am told he swore loyalty to your Dragon Blood, did he not?" Zoltan nods at the half-awake demon dragging his feet to his room. His guard duty must've just finished because not even the darkened hallway with its flickering flames is able to hide the tired slump of his shoulders and the strained lines on his face.

"That means you can rough him up, maybe, but you will not hurt him even if you lose control," Zoltan continues after the demon clicks his door shut behind him. "The ways of the Fae are familiar to me, although I cannot say I understand them completely."

"All of you have been around me at some point when I wasn't myself." Gnawing on the inside of my cheek, I avoid looking at him. "I haven't hurt any of you." A pained yelp echoes in my head from my memories, making me physically flinch. "Well, I hurt Leo, but only once, and it wasn't intentional. I acted on instinct. That was because Fenrir forced the damn thing to show up and take control."

"You will learn to control it with time." Giving my hand a reassuring squeeze, he pushes the door to his room open. "You still think of the two of you as separate beings. You are not."

"And you sound like Myst right now."

Butterflies erupt in my stomach when Zoltan's bed looms in front of my eyes. My feet falter at the door and the vampire freezes, the unnatural stillness of his entire being raising the short hairs at the back of my neck. Panic accelerates my breathing. I'm about to turn around and bolt out of here before I do something stupid. As if reading my mind, Zoltan releases my hand and saunters deeper inside his room, ignoring me like I'm not even here.

It helps.

Be it manipulation or his way of actually being a decent male and putting me at ease, the focused way he is moving around his personal space is enough that I close the door behind me, leaning on it with my arms folded across my chest. Being the hypocrite I am, my eyes roam over his body noticing the way his black t-shirt strains over his bulging biceps, and the way his pants wrap around his powerful thighs with each step. Dragging a chair to the middle of the room, he climbs on it and lifts both arms to the ceiling. The hem of his shirt rides up, giving me a glimpse of his abs. My mouth dries up. I'm smacked out of my lust-filled thoughts when orange rays drape over his body like he just flicked a light on. My eyes jerk up to the ceiling.

"What the fuck?" At my shout, Zoltan looks down at me, the corners of his lips tilted into a mischievous smile.

I watch in horror when he shoves his hand inside the gaping hole of the open compartment where the tentacles of some creature are writhing hungrily in the air. *'I should not be thinking about octopus ever again.'* Chiding myself internally, I stare openmouthed at the rows of sharp teeth on the disgusting appendages. As soon as they sink into his skin, their frantic movement stops and they disappear in the hole, which leaves me wondering if I actually saw them or if I'm hallucinating.

Lifting on the balls of his feet, Zoltan shuffles around the inside of his ceiling, pulling his hand out a moment later with the book gripped in his fingers. With a triumphant grin, he pulls the moving compartment back in place—thank fuck—hiding whatever that thing was from view. Jumping off the chair, the graceful way his body moves distracts me from my frozen horror just enough to jumpstart my brain.

"What was that?" My finger stabs the air pointing at the ceiling.

"I'm not sure what they are called." Zoltan brushes off the cover of the book, puffing a cloud of dust in the air. "Fenrir found it for me when he visited his home. They are not intelligent, so they are deadly, but smart enough to not harm the one that feeds them. Perfect for the protection of things you don't want anyone to find."

"In the ceiling?" I sound like an idiot, but I still can't get over what I just saw.

"If you break in here for something that you know I'm hiding"—He comes to stand in front of me with the book held at chest level between us— "where would you look for it?"

I blink stupidly at him.

"You'd search the walls, the floor, under, behind, and inside everything you see." He tucks a stray hair behind my ear, his hand lingering on my face before he drops it to his side. "Only one in a million would go poking around in the ceiling."

My gaze darts to the spot above our heads, the smooth surface not showing any sign of being disturbed. There are no lines, cracks, or bumps on it. It's white, flat, and unblemished. The fact that I was hiding the serpentine stone and my daggers in the floor is not lost on me. When I look back at him, the book is lowered to his side and Zoltan is standing much closer than before.

Too close for my sanity.

"You feel better knowing the book is still in our possession?" His voice is conversational but there is no mistaking the burning intensity in his blue eyes.

I swallow thickly, wetting my dry mouth.

"We are missing something." It's a struggle to keep my brain out of the gutter. "All the attacks, everything that has happened so far tells me Roberti is making us chase our tails. Something is happening right under our noses while all we do is remove everyone he is willing to sacrifice to keep us away." My brother being one of them. I don't say it, but it hangs like an anvil between us.

He flicks his gaze between mine, the hunger slightly subdued. "What are you thinking?"

"That that's the actual problem." When a line forms between his eyebrows, I push aside my pride. "Roberti knows exactly what I'm thinking and how I think. All of you keep saying I'm the wild card, but the problem is he knows how I react and how to push all my buttons. We are playing into his hand."

"You will let me take the lead?" If I wasn't so unnerved by his nearness, I would've laughed at his shocked face.

"I suck at being a team player or a follower, Zoltan." A humorless laugh bubbles out of my chest. "Hell, I couldn't even play nice with any partner I had in the agency because my basic survival instinct has its wires crossed somewhere. I'm all for keeping myself breathing unless there is someone that can't fight for themselves. In that case, all my will to live goes down the drain. I don't think, I act."

"Because you had no one to do that for you." His words are like a slap in the face, and I feel the sting all the way to my heart.

"But that's not true, is it?" Tears prickle the corners of

my eyes, but I push them away with determination. "You protected me from those shadows."

"I should've been protecting you a long time before that." A muscle jumps in his jaw and he takes a step closer. "I should've been there to watch over you. I wasn't then, but I am now."

My back hits the door when I try to get away from him. "I can take care of myself."

"You can." The thump when the book hits the floor at my feet makes me jump. "But you don't have to anymore."

"I don't need ..." His mouth crashes on mine and steals my words.

When he lets me come up for air, a dazed feeling swims in my head and my eyes have lost all focus. It takes a long minute to snap out of it and when I do, I scowl at him.

"I don't need you to protect me. I need to stop being impulsive so I can beat that asshole at his own game." I growl the words through clenched teeth.

"For that, you need someone else to take the lead." His gaze flicks from my eyes to my lips and back. "You keep saying you are not afraid, and I believe you"—The smile threatening to curl my lips gets gold when he continues talking— "when it comes to Roberti. When it comes to me, you are scared shitless."

I gape at him, more because he used the word "shitless" than anything else. I've noticed modern terms elude his speech, yet lately he's been using more and more of them. I'd love to take credit for bringing the centuries-old vampire to modern times, but I don't dare say it because I know he will stop just to spite me. He loves pushing my buttons, too.

"I don't fear you, Daywalker." Jutting my chin, I stare down my nose at him.

One side of his mouth cocks up and he shows me a hint

of a fang. My heart jumps in my throat then plummets to my feet. The frenzied butterflies in my stomach must've gotten drunk because they are going nuts and making me feel dizzy. Either the floor is moving or I'm swaying on my feet. If anyone asks the floor is unsteady, and I'll die with that story on my lips if I have too.

"Are you sure, Love?" One of Zoltan's eyebrows arches up.

"I am not afraid of you." Saying each word slowly to drill it in his thick head, I gulp when his smile grows.

"Prove it." The dare is a primal growl from his chest.

Ah, fuck. I'm doomed.

Chapter Ten

Zoltan spears his fingers through my hair, which prevents me from escaping his hungry kiss. Not that the idea ever crosses my mind. My lips part eagerly for his tongue and I melt to his chest while he devours my mouth. The hard press of the door on my back disappears and he leads me backward, both of us stumbling and tripping over each other's feet in our haste. Releasing my hair, his fingers find the edge of my shirt and yank it over my head in one sharp tug. We part our lips for a second and his t-shirt joins mine on the floor. Everything he said a second ago to piss me off flies out the window to join the brainless birds chirping on the trees. Maybe I should go join them too. It'll be the healthier option for sure.

Forgetting all the reasons why I shouldn't do this, why I don't deserve it, my hands glide over his chest and shoulders, my fingertips bumping all the ridges of the defined muscles on his torso. Zoltan is a work of art not meant for either mortal or immortal eyes. I might not deserve to enjoy it, but I'll take it regardless. It's one step closer to heartbreak and I'm willingly going to take it. The back of my knees hit the bed and I pitch backward, sinking into the mattress.

Looming above me with mussed hair and kiss-swollen lips like some deity I ought to worship, his gaze crawls over my exposed skin and spread legs from where he is standing. My entire focus zeros in on his hand when he slowly—very slowly—starts unbuttoning his pants. A pathetic whimper passes my lips when those pants hang loose enough on his hips to reveal his V lines, and the fact that he is not wearing anything else underneath them almost makes me come undone. Leaning down, his deft fingers make quick work of my own pants, yanking them down my legs with jerky movements. I should be embarrassed because of how wet I am, the inside of my thighs sleek with it, but I'm beyond any rational thought right now. I'd love nothing more than to blame my craving for him on Zoltan's mind powers, to convince myself that he's the one making me a pathetic mess. I could really, but I'll own up to this because not even a mind fuck can make me as desperate for him as I am making myself.

Kicking away the pile of our clothing at his feet, Zoltan's fully naked body straightens and his cock juts out between his legs. I moan low in my throat when he wraps his fingers around his erection, gliding his hand up and down and torturing me. Fisting the sheets so I don't reach for him, I pant, moving my hips in hopes to press my thighs together and get some relief from the building pressure there. My channel is throbbing, grasping empty air when all I need is to be filled.

"Tell me you want me." Zoltan's voice is much deeper, the primal edge to it making my spine stiffen.

"We gonna fuck, or you want to chat?" Inside my head

a voice is screaming, '*Please say fuck, please say fuck*', but I glare at him with a dare.

He folds his body over me, holding himself above me with one arm. I almost cry from joy because he has finally decided to stop talking and fill the emptiness I feel. My legs fall further open when his fingers press between my lower lips, stroking up and down to spread the wetness. His face is close to mine but too far to reach if I want to kiss him. And I really, really want to kiss him. When two thick fingers enter me, my eyes roll to the back of my head and my hips rise off the bed.

"Tell me you want me, Francesca." There is a lisp to his words from the fangs that are peeking under his upper lip.

"I want you to fuck me." Breathlessly, I moan the words, my hips pumping in sync with his hand.

"Not my cock, Love." I hate the amusement in his voice. "Tell me you want *me*."

His fingers stretch and swivel, the heel of his palm pressing on my button just enough to drive me insane but nothing else. When he thumps it harder, my back bows off the bed and a keening sound rips from my lips. Zoltan dips his head and catches one nipple in the hot depths of his mouth, his tongue lashing the stiff peak in tandem with the movement of his fingers.

Releasing my tender breast with a pop, he lifts his head and pins me under his hungry gaze. "Tell me you want this bond we have as much as I do."

"You are a manipulative asshole." Gasping the words, I can't stop my hips from moving.

A third finger joins the other two and makes me nothing more than a writhing mess under him as the sheets twist around me.

"You are scared to care, but you want it." His knowing eyes are a dagger in my heart. "Tell me you want it."

The hand disappears from between my legs and my eyes snap open. I didn't even know I had them closed. My breath lodges in my throat when I see Zoltan's somber face, his eyes searching mine. Heart hammering my ribcage, I stare back at him, a lump the size of a fist forming at the sadness in those blue depths. Tears prickle in my eyes, wetting the edges of my lashes.

"You are a heartbreak waiting to happen, Zoltan." Choking it out, I swallow thickly. "Why are you doing this?"

"I will not hurt you, Francesca."

For the first time, he lets me see him without any of the masks he usually wears to prevent anyone from guessing what he is thinking. He allowed me to see his hurt at Daren's house when I was being a bitch and trying to push him away. It was more of a knee-jerk reaction that caused him to slip up and give me that glimpse. But it was not like this. What I see right now takes my breath away. The unstoppable, impenetrable Daywalker who has always been larger than life is showing his vulnerability to me. A half-blood who isn't even worthy to be in the same space as him, let alone naked in his bed. It unfurls something inside me I didn't know was slowly strangling my heart.

"You will." A treacherous tear rolls over, making a rivulet down my face before soaking in my hair. He watches it with acute fascination.

"Never." Cupping my face, he rubs his thumb over my cheekbone wiping the wet trail of the tear. "Tell me you want the bond and I will prove you wrong, Love."

I stay quiet for long enough to see hurt flash through his eyes. Shifting, he lifts higher above me and panic grips me in an iron fist. I already feel the loss of his nearness, the knowledge that I will never touch him freely ripping my insides to shreds.

But he doesn't stand up.

There is a nudge of the blunt head of his cock bumping my button a moment before he enters me with one swift jerk of his hips. He sinks in to the hilt, and although I'm wet and ready for him, it gives me a delicious burn bordering between pleasure and pain. My mouth opens in a silent scream when Zoltan doesn't pause to give me time to adjust to him. Grabbing one of my thighs, he lifts my leg higher up his torso to give him a different angle. Sinking in deeper than before, his hips piston between my legs.

I meet him thrust for thrust. Wrapping my arms around his shoulders, I claw at his back until he growls deep in his chest. I feel him everywhere, an all-consuming presence threatening to devour me whole, yet it's not enough. His mouth crashes over mine hungrily and I open for him, our tongues gliding together in a dance older than time. Something is still missing, though, and the aching need leaves me feeling hollow.

"I want it." I hear my voice, my lips moving without permission as soon as he releases my mouth from the scorching kiss.

All his movement stops, the intensity of the way he is searching my face sending a shiver up and down my spine. Goosebumps pop up all over my arms and legs, yet he doesn't say anything, only stares at me like a breathing statue above me. That is not the full truth. His cock is throbbing and pulsing inside me and my channel clenches around it.

"I want the bond." Repeating it more steadily, my hands

caress his back, the tips of my fingers grazing the smooth skin. "I want you." He is still silent, and my nerves get the better of me. "I still want your cock too, so if you would move …"

I have enough time to gasp before his arm snakes around my waist and he lifts me off the bed. He palms the back of my head with his free hand, leaving me suspended in the air while practically sitting in his lap. All I can do is hold on to his shoulders while my nails dig into his skin as he starts pounding his hips between my legs with renewed vigor. The connection I have with Zoltan hits me like a battering ram when he opens it, spreading scorching heat through my entire being.

That was what was missing, I think before all thoughts drift into some unknown space.

All I know is the coiling pressure building in my lower belly. I can feel my own, and Zoltan's too. It brings everything to such intense levels I'm not sure I'll be sane after it's over. An undeniable urge surges through me, and on instinct alone, I grab his head and yank it to the side. I realize what I'm doing when my fangs sink deep in his neck and the warm gush of his blood slides down my throat. If possible, Zoltan's thrusts become faster, harder. The coil tightens inside me, making me scratch at his shoulder hard enough to leave trails of shredded skin behind. Red rivulets trickle between my fingers and down his back. He snarls like a feral beast, his thick cock swelling inside me and filling me to bursting as it bumps the mouth of my womb with each jerk of his hips.

That's when he strikes.

Zoltan's fangs sink into my neck to complete the blood exchange, and a supernova explodes in me. Stars burst behind my closed eyelids at the first drag of his mouth. It feels like each suction of his lips is connected to my nub and he is sucking on it instead of my neck. The second pull brings rainbow colors swirling among the bursting stars. I gulp his blood greedily, but I'm lost in the insanity of the pleasure. The third sends me hurling into a void where there is nothing but darkness and so many strong emotions my entire body goes numb.

Zoltan keeps thrusting. I feel him even in this place where I'm weightless. I can't remember my name, but I remember his. All I know in this void of pleasure is him. It lasts seconds, minutes, or maybe an eternity, but it changes something fundamental in me. The roar coming from him is somewhere in the distance, but it merges with my voice as I scream his name.

A thick bright cord drags me back to reality and I know it's Zoltan, the bond we somehow created bringing me back to him like two magnets being pulled together. It's much stronger now, this connection we share. It should freak me out, but all I can do is breathe as I feel his lips on my sweaty skin. Zoltan is still holding me in his arms, breathing harshly but peppering soft, gentle kisses over my face, neck, and shoulders. Any place his lips can reach.

"Thank you." I feel his words more than I can hear them.

"Don't thank me." He silences me with the press of his mouth on mine. "You might regret it later." I finish after he moves away.

"I just want you to trust me, Love." The small smile playing on his lips melts me into a puddle. I'm a fool, I know. "Leave everything else to me."

"Tough chance that, but you can keep dreaming." I smirk at his glower as I hang boneless in his embrace. "It's a nice pipe dream to have."

"I hate when I taste another male's blood in you." His jaw tightens but he unclenches it with effort. I keep my mouth shut so I don't have to explain why I have Daren's blood inside me.

Shuffling on his knees, he scoots us to the middle of the bed before lowering me on it and curling around me protectively. It's enough to bring new tears to my eyes. The only thing stopping me from crying is his cock still as hard as steel inside me. My channel clenches around it and Zoltan growls in his chest.

"You will be okay, Francesca."

Burying his face in my neck, he takes a deep breath as if he wants to drown in the scent of my skin. My own nostrils are full of his sinful aroma, and I know I'll smell him for days even if he is not around. The room is drenched in the scent of sex and sweaty skin, which prevents me from opening my eyelids fully. The Daywalker doesn't do anything half assed. He takes all or nothing, and I folded under his demands willingly. *You only live once,* I tell myself before that snarky asshole that's also me reminds me, *It will be a very long miserable existence if you get hurt.*

I shove it away.

"What are you thinking?" Zoltan murmurs sleepily.

"We need to figure out how the Board is connected to Roberti." I can't even convince myself that the problem we have is on my mind.

Zoltan snorts, tightening his arms around me. "I did a piss poor job if you are thinking about the Board or Roberti with my cock still inside you."

"You did a great job, trust me." Petting his bicep, my channel clenches around his hardness as if it has a mind of its own.

"Mmmm … I think I'll need to try harder." He mockingly snarls against my hair, raising goosebumps on my arms.

"No, you—" A moan is wrenched out of me when he swivels his hips.

"I am far from finished with you." His dark chuckle gets lost in my screams.

Chapter Eleven

Holding my breath, I watch the group of mages disappear around the corner, their voices carrying long after the animated chatty Cathy's are gone. What everyone forgot to mention when Myst was training me to control my aura was the fact that we don't sense it either. The mages just proved it by passing by me without blinking an eye.

A small smile tilts my lips, excitement rushing through my veins. Stepping out of the shadowed corner, I dart a glance left and right to make sure I'm alone in the forbidden part of the academy where only the Board and those invited are allowed to step foot. The expensive tastes of those old farts must be supported somehow, and if my assumptions are correct it has everything to do with a damned demigod.

Tenebris bumps into my leg, shifting restlessly with a bored expression on his giant face. I guess he is not impressed by my skulking skills. Then again, when is a feline impressed unless you have food or give it scratches under the chin. Which I'm doing right now, eliciting a soft purr from the enormous panther. His eyelids lower and his jaw juts out slightly to guide my wiggling fingers, at least until he realizes what I'm doing and glowers at me after jerking his head back.

I grin like a fool.

"Let's go." Breathing the words for his ears only, my soundless feet carry me further into the wide foyer of the Board wing.

The large chandelier hanging on the tall ceiling rocks gently from the nonexistent breeze, the diamonds on it casting glittering rainbow colors where the flames reflect on it. Like twinkling stars, the precious stones and gold and silver accents placed everywhere wink at me as I dart from one place to the next, Tenebris hot on my heels.

Okay, so I lied.

A little.

In my defense, just because I owned up to my shit and told Zoltan that I want the bond we somehow forged does not mean I'm okay with waiting to hear what our next move will be. So, like every smart female—or stupid depending how you look at it—here I am attempting to spy on the old farts. They've been pretty inventive in their tactics to stay out of my way, only popping in when it suits them. It's time I take the game to them. All I want is to see if I can overhear something they don't want anyone to know. Like them talking about Roberti, or my early death. Anything really. If one or all three of them die in the process?

Well ... oops.

I'm done playing defense and watching over my shoulder wherever I go, and I'm really sick of sleeping with one eye open.

"Two can play the game of cat and mouse," I murmur under my breath while glancing at Tenebris. "Pun intended." One of his ears flicks my way but that's all the reaction I get.

There are not many places where you can hide in the open, especially having the shifter with me, but I manage to get near the ornate double doors where I was "invited" by the old farts for a party in my honor as Fenrir's imaginary fiancé. I have no idea where they usually go, but at least it's a place to start my search. Not paying attention, I almost faceplant and sprawl into the open when Tenebris cuts me off just as I'm about to get my ass inside.

Wind milling my arms, I jerk back and glare at the stupid feline. "What in the fates is the matter with you." Hissing, I kick his hind leg.

Ignoring my outrage, he keeps shoving me back the way we came. I can either make a lot of noise by arguing with him or follow him to wherever he plans to take me. Grinding my teeth, I let him hoard me back until he stops near a plain wooden door that looks out of place against the luxury surrounding us. I saw it when we passed by, but I thought it was a side door to a stairway or something, so I didn't pay too much attention. When muffled voices reach my ears, I scurry closer without much prompting from Tenebris.

Plastering myself to the door, I press my ear against it as hard as I can in the hopes I will hear who is in there and what they are saying. It is much easier to eavesdrop on the demons from the roof than it is to listen through a wooden door. It might look plain but it's obviously thick. The Board doesn't do anything half assed when it comes to hiding their secrets.

I almost jump out of my skin when a hand wraps around my mouth, silencing the shriek that gets stuck in my throat. On impulse, my elbow jerks back fast as lightening, and a satisfying grunt reaches my buzzing ears. Lifting my knee up, I step as hard as I can on the person's foot, the heel of my boot grinding the bones as I twist around the moment their hold loosens.

And I come face to face with a pissed-off Zoltan.

A muscle jumps in his carved- of-stone face.

Grabbing me by the upper arm, he yanks me along with him the way I came, the fast clip of his boots on the fishbone floors clipping like whips lashing exposed flash. Stunned, I follow him while I peer over my shoulder at the simple door, my curiosity battling against the knowledge that I better do what he wants me to do. I know there is a lecture coming, too. That jerk Tenebris bolted out of here like a coward, leaving me to deal with the furious Daywalker on my own.

As soon as we are out of the Board's wing of the academy, Zoltan abruptly stops and jerks me around so I'm facing him.

"What do you think you are doing?" His clipped words are spoken through clenched teeth.

"What does it look like?" Tugging my arm out of his grasp, I take a deep breath. *Don't piss him off more than he already is, Franky. He will follow you around and you won't be able to do shit,* I tell myself to calm my anger. "I haven't been around this place much. I was sightseeing."

"Sightseeing?" he repeats, but that one word also says, 'You either think I'm an idiot or you are stupid.' I see it in his scowling eyes.

"Yeah, I was bored." Folding my arms over my chest, I jut my chin up.

"Snooping and trying to get yourself killed is what you were doing." Seething, Zoltan leans threateningly toward me. A shiver slithers up and down my spine. So much for calming down.

"There is nothing wrong with snooping to hear what those assholes are hiding." Shoving him on the shoulders with both hands to get him out of my face, which doesn't move him at all, I glare at him. How in the worlds did he find me so fast? It's that damn bond, I know it. It serves me right to mix business with pleasure. "Are we going to sit around and wait for them to come to us and confess they are working with Roberti?"

His gaze flicks through mine and I'll give anything to know what he is thinking. *He might be regretting the bond right now,* a stupid voice hisses in my head, and it sends a punch to the center of my chest. I grind my teeth so hard I think I might break a molar or something. Zoltan's nostrils flare, but he takes a step back and relaxes his shoulders. It's fascinating to see the effort it takes him not to strangle me like he wants to at the moment. Some idiotic part of my brain is rejoicing at the sight.

"There are better ways of doing it, Love." There is still a frustrated growl in his tone, but his hand is gentle when he takes my fingers in his. "Come, I need you to hear something."

"I was about to hear something until you butted your nose into things you shouldn't." Grumbling, I fall in step with him.

"This might get you upset but I need you to keep an open mind and hear us out." He ignores me like I haven't spoken.

"Oh, goody! I can't wait." He flicks an irritated look at my chirp, but he keeps walking with his head held high.

Something about the way he holds himself stiff and coiled as if ready to pounce and tackle me to the ground at any moment sets off alarms that blare in my head. So focused on the vibes coming off him, I'm not even paying attention to where he is taking me. My feet will follow Zoltan to my doom it seems. Not that the rest of me wouldn't the second I sense him near. "Our ovaries will be our doom," my mother used to say. In her case it takes on a whole different meaning, especially if more siblings I never knew about start popping up. With that reminder, everything screeches to a halt. My feet plant on the floor, my heels digging in.

"If you are …"

I don't finish the sentence. Zoltan opens a door, shoving me inside and slamming it shut behind him. Spreading his legs shoulder width apart, his arms cross over his wide chest where he blocks my exit. There is a stubborn set to his mouth, his full lips thinned out from being pressed together in determination. Silence greets my ears, but I can feel eyes stabbing me between my shoulder blades. If I want to get out of here I'll have to fight the damn vampire, and I'm not sure I can win. Isn't that a bitch slap to my ego?

Someone clears their throat.

Hands clenched into fists at my sides, I slowly turn and give the most dangerous person in the room my back. Somewhere in the back of my mind I'm well aware of the significance of my gesture, even if I didn't hear the approving soft growl coming from Zoltan, which is something I can't think about right now. Not with everyone watching me as if I'm about to lose my shit.

I am, but that's beside the point.

"I'm listening." Deciding to get it over with instead of acting like a child having a tantrum, I steel my spine and focus on the wall so I don't have to make eye contact with anyone.

"She was skulking around the Board wing," Zoltan, the snitch, tells the room like we are two-year old's and he is hoping to get me in trouble.

"Investigating." Turning to him over my shoulder, I make sure he sees I'm not impressed. "There is a difference."

"Did you find something, Hellion?" Fenrir is sitting ram rod straight like he has swallowed a stick, his chair shifted to the side of the table and one ankle crossed over his knee. Every bit the royal Fae, this one.

"I was interrupted." Waving off the fake interest about what I did or did not find, I swirl my hand at no one in particular to hurry this torture along. "What is it that I need to hear?"

"I'm sorry." My heart shrivels in my chest, and I can feel the blood draining from my face at my mother's soft words. "I was beside myself, so lost in my grief for your brother. I should not have said those words."

"I deserved it, so there is nothing you need to apologize for apart from hiding the fact that he existed." My nails dig into my palms and I feel blood dribbling from them. I'll bury my fingers to my knuckles just to hide the fact that my hands are shaking. "If that is all, I have things to do and people to kill."

"Francesca Drake, you listen to me." She moves around the table where she was standing next to Fenrir. "I've done many things I regret, but I'm trying to atone for those wrongs."

"And you needed an audience to do it?" Pointing at everyone listening quietly to this drama, I hate that my voice breaks.

Even Argoz, the ghoul, is here, pale as a sheet as he yanks on the damn collar of his shirt. Leo and Daren stand close together, leaning on the side of the wall while watching with unreadable faces. Astara has her back turned to us and is staring out the window. I really don't blame her for not wanting to look at me.

Tears shimmer in my mother's eyes, but she lifts her chin proudly. "If you have forgotten, I am a pure blood."

"Don't remind me."

"And I have access to the elusive Board that you do not." She glares.

"They know you are my mother," I point out the obvious.

"They don't." Astara finally turns, her gaze eerily similar to Zoltan's as it hones in on me. "When everything settled, I told them she is a cousin we met up with in the human world."

"And you think they bought the lie? I'm sure they are working with Roberti, even though I can't prove it yet. They know exactly who she is."

"Or they don't know *yet*, so maybe we shouldn't be wasting time." Fenrir sighs and gracefully straights to his full height from his chair.

"Wasting how?" I'm missing something here. I can almost taste it.

"Silas invited me for dinner later tonight." My mother dares me to say something and I bite my tongue so I don't take the bait. "I've been trying to earn his trust so he feels comfortable sharing plans that he otherwise wouldn't."

"I bet it's a real chore for you, Mother." Ignoring the disapproving expression on Fenrir's face, I keep my eyes locked on hers.

"I want all of them dead as much as you, you insolent child," she hisses. "That was my child that died under their influence."

"I was the one wielding the blade." Bile burns the back of my throat, but somehow, I push through. "It was my hand that took his life."

"And they will pay for that too." I visibly flinch from the venom spitting out of her mouth. "I will make it right, Franky, if it's the last thing I do. Mark my words."

Between bawling my eyes out at hearing her say my nickname and sinking deeper into the numbness, I choose the latter. "And you want me to do exactly what in the meantime? Sit around and wait?" My gaze travels across their faces, apart from Zoltan who is still standing like an unmovable rock at my back.

"No, you will snoop." Leo grins at me, his mouth cocked to the side to reveal a dimple on his cheek.

"She likes to call it investigating." There is no mistaking the amusement in Zoltan's voice.

"Snoop where?" All my stress and anger are forgotten at the idea of actually doing something.

"Ah, you'll have to wait and see, Hellion." Fenrir chuckles and I get a really bad feeling about this. "Where is the fun in telling you everything?"

"This will be a disaster." Daren grumbles, voicing exactly what I'm thinking.

Chapter Twelve

"You know you looming like that defies the purpose of snooping, right?" I shuffle my feet, which are itching to get away from Zoltan.

"Investigating." His intent stare dares me to argue with him.

"It defies the purpose of investigating." Pushing the words through clenched teeth, I want to slap the amused twinkle from his eye. "You should've gone with Fenrir. Silas is going to kill my mother before any of you realize what's happening."

We split into pairs to get more things done, according to Zoltan. Astara, who seems upset with me, left with Fenrir to keep an eye on my mother's dinner date. Leo and Daren went to the human realm to find out if Myst has any information we can use. To my greatest joy, Tenebris got stuck with Argoz and they were keeping watch over the portal. The panther was so pissed he couldn't come with me that he almost bit Argoz's leg off when the ghoul walked pass him. Because I laughed at the shifter, karma bit me in the ass.

I got saddled with Zoltan.

"You don't trust Fenrir?" Cocking one eyebrow, he steps closer to me.

"It's my mother I don't trust. On the best of days, I have to restrain myself from throttling her. Have you met the female?" Sticking my head around the corner, I scan the deserted hallway. Why aren't there more people walking around?

"Sophia is just like any typical female vampire." Zoltan dismisses my comment with a flick of his hand. "They feel entitled."

"They are entitled." Which is the problem that started all this crap.

If vampires didn't think the moon shined from their ass then Roberti would've had a harder time enlisting help from people. Add to that the invincibility the bloodsuckers get when becoming Daywalkers and you have the perfect reason for people to want them out of the picture. I get Roberti's hook. He is using everyone's feeling of repression to realize his plans. I don't agree with it, but I sure as all hells get it. Inching to the side, I slip past Zoltan and move down the hall.

"If you were Andrius, which Titan would you try to release from his prison?" I ask the vampire when he falls in step with me. "I sound like a broken record but that has been nagging me from the moment I set eyes on the damn book."

Zoltan chews on the question for a long moment, and just when I think he won't answer, he shrugs a shoulder. "Does it matter? He will not be freeing anything."

"I think it matters a lot." Offering a tightlipped smile to

a shifter walking past, I wait until I don't feel their presence anymore. "It might give us a clue at what Roberti is planning to achieve with all this."

"He wants war."

"I have no idea in which dimension you've been living, but if he simply wants war, he could have it without all the shit he's been trying to pull." The more I talk the more right it feels. "This is personal to him. I feel it in my bones. I just can't figure out what prize awaits him at the end of the line."

"He is a demigod of war, Love." With a hand at the small of my back, he guides me up the wide stairway to the second floor. "The bloodlust in him is as strong as any feral vampire. Just the thought of battle boils their blood."

He says what I already know about any demigod, what all of us have heard about the bloodlines of the gods. But try as I may, it still doesn't feel right. Andrius betrayed me and manipulated me, yes. But even despite my fear of upsetting him, I've been observing him for years. The demigod might be hotblooded, but he is also cunning and smart.

And greedy for power.

My boots scuff the stairs as we climb higher up, the misty smell of the libraries on the third floor already filling my nostrils halfway to that level. My ex-boss always wanted to be on top of the ladder. And for everyone else to know he is at the top, too. Power hungry, merciless, and as I found out the hard way, with no conscience. A picture of a triangular symbol pops up in my mind's eye, axes crossed and a lightning splitting them in half. The emblem on the hood of the hunter's car floats in front of my distant gaze.

"This way." Zoltan's voice pulls me out of my thoughts, and I look around the unfamiliar area of the academy.

"Where are we?" There is a sharp scent in the air. It burns my nose, so I rub it with the back of my hand.

"Tonight is the full moon so all the shifters will be outside. Including the Board members," Zoltan explains as we pass by many closed doors. "The vampire is busy entertaining your mother, so that only leaves the mage with nothing to do."

We stop before a withered door, the wood covered with scratches and cracks like something has been pounding on it on a regular basis. I eye it skeptically, doubting any of the old farts will be seen dead near something so cheap and used. If there were jewels or gold on it, they'd be all over it I'm sure. *Soren is no better in his golden halls,* my mind reminds me, but I push it away. My Dragon Blood craves shiny things too, but you don't see me turning a blind eye to people dying for it. The ancient Fae has much more important things to worry about. Like feeding his life to this place just so the jerks can try to kill each other.

"Nothing to do but magic." Zoltan pulls my eyes from the door to his face.

"Here?" I don't hide the doubt in my voice.

"It's reinforced with wards in case any spells go wrong. The wards will make sure the place isn't blown up, so when things don't go his way, this is where he normally hides." His palm presses on the cracked door testing it for something. He jerks his hand back and shakes it to the side. "We should wait a moment."

No sooner than he is done talking, a crash of shattering glass comes from behind the closed door. Adrenaline spikes in my veins and the monstrosity inside me perks, the magic answering immediately in short, sharp pulses. Zoltan steps back, pushing me aside with a hand pressed to the center of my chest. A pained shout reaches my ears and my knees bend slightly in reaction to it. Ramming his shoulder at the door, Zoltan bounces back before repeating it again. I hold my breath, but after the fourth time without breaking the door, I grab hold of his arm.

"Let's try together." My words come out shaky from the heartbeat thumping in my throat.

He gives me a jerky nod and we line up next to each other. Pain zips from my shoulder all the way to my tailbone when I collide with the frail-looking door. Looks could be deceiving and it's about time I learn that little lesson. Taking two steps back, I stiffen right before both Zoltan and I body slam the warded wood as hard as we can. Splinters burst from it on all sides, the sharp edges of the broken door shredding my arm and hip.

I forget all about the pain when I see the old mage facing off with a shifter that doesn't look right. His body is half transformed, fur sprouting in places and doubling his size, but that's where it stops. The shift is not completed so he looks like a thing of nightmares, a creature between a man and a beast. And that's not the most disturbing thing. His eyes glow a deep amber color I've never seen on any shifter before, and saliva dribbles down his chin from long, sharp teeth on a too-human face. The tall window behind him is broken in the middle like somehow the beast jumped three stories high through it. But that's impossible, right?

Zoltan doesn't debate what he is seeing. Bouncing off the balls of his feet, he throws himself past the mage at the shifter taking him to the ground. That's when I see the hunter standing behind him, clutching two of the metal stars in his hands. Without a thought, I tackle the mage and roll with him on the floor over sharp pieces of broken glass. The old male grunts but otherwise doesn't make a sound. A whistling noise and a dull thump tell me the weapons were discharged but missed their mark. That motherfucker was going to nail me with it if he got lucky. Colors come alive around me and my vision shifts to adjust to my dragon sight. Jerking my head up, I lock eyes with the hunter and grin at his widening stare.

"My turn." The chuckle coming out of my mouth scares the shit out of me, but I'm already shoving off the mage and jumping to my feet. "Stay down." I stab a finger at his upturned face without taking my eyes off the hunter. I see him nod shakily from the corner of my eye before I side-step away from his sprawled body and he crabwalks away to a corner.

The hunter snaps out of his stupor and moves until both of us circle each other. I keep him as far from the mage as possible without having my head ripped off my shoulders by the swinging fists and claws between Zoltan and the beast. Slaps of flesh hitting flesh fill the room, mingling with the crunching of glass under my feet. There is a fleeting thought that it might be the stupid initiation making me want to protect the mage even though I want nothing more than to see all three of them dead, but it's gone in a second when I focus on the hunter's soulless irises.

"You attack an old male when he is not looking," I purr at the hunter. "Let's see how tough you are when you are expected."

Hatred burns on his face and, pulling out a long dagger, he slashes at my chest. My back bends back, the sharp metal passing half an inch from my body. Using the momentum, I twist to the side and my hand shoots out to latch onto his outstretched arm. Yanking with my full body weight, I use him to regain my balance while he ends up somersaulting, his arm breaking in my hold before he slams into the ground on his back. I pounce on his chest with both knees, the crunch of his ribs like music to my ears. The hunter's mouth is open, but the air has been pushed out of his lungs so his screams are silent. Bending down, I bring my face nose to nose with his.

"Whatever made you think it was smart to come in my home?" The beast Zoltan is fighting howls in pain, which has my lips stretching into a wider smile. The hunter's eyes are about to pop out of his head, his red, bloodshot capillaries spreading through the whites like cobwebs.

Sharp searing pain spreads through my side and makes my eyes cross. I feel the blade the hunter pulls out from between my ribs, his shoulder tensing so he can stab me again. That's what I get for talking instead of killing the fucker. My hand wraps around his throat as my fangs drop from my gums. All the slaps, grunts, and howls are gone, the silence around me thundering in my ears. The horror on the hunter's face should disturb me, but I'm way past rationality at this point. His screams only fuel my insanity while I rip him apart piece by piece like I have all the time in the world.

Strong hands wrap around my shoulders and lift me off the pulverized pile underneath me. My feral snarl and snapping jaws do not faze Zoltan one bit. He holds me in front of him at arm's length, his face stoic and his shoulders relaxed. Those blue eyes are entirely focused on mine and the bond we share keeps pulsing warmth through my limbs. I didn't realize how frozen I felt inside until this moment. My struggling stops and I blink fast, my vision returning to normal. Acid crawls up my throat when I feel blood covering my face and dribbling down my chin.

"Breathe," Zoltan commands, and I automatically obey him because I'll hurl the contents of my stomach all over him otherwise. "That's it, Love. Just breathe." He kneads my shoulders, the soothing movement calming the panic that's trying to overwhelm me.

"Zoltan"—The old mage lifts off the floor, pale and obviously shaken, but keeps his back plastered on the wall—"thank the fates you heard my call."

"You screamed like a little bitch, asshole. That wasn't a call," I retort without thinking. Zoltan's lips twitch at the corners.

"Miss Drake." The old fart swallows thickly, and I can hear his heart fluttering in his chest, every second beat skipped. "My gratitude for your assistance."

"I'd say you are welcome but that would be a lie. I just hate hunters more than I hate you." My head tilts to the side. "Scratch that. I hate you the same. Maybe I should end you now too and get it over and done with."

Zoltan gives my shoulders a squeeze before taking his hands away. I miss his touch immediately, my blood rushing through my veins faster from the lack of his warmth. The bond strengthens, caressing me from the inside. I have to ask him to teach me how he is doing this, making me feel him as if we have physical contact while he is a few feet away.

"What Francesca is saying is"—The vampire turns his cold stare on the mage— "there is a reason they sent these two to kill you. You either didn't do your job properly or you are standing in the way." The mage gulps and his Adams apple bobs on his neck. "Which one is it?"

"I would never betray this academy." The old fart squares his shoulders. "I have sworn an oath."

"A lot of good it did us, your stupid oath." I snort ungracefully and he glares at me.

"Which one is it?" Zoltan repeats his question, his voice sharper than a blade cutting through the air.

"I can't ..." the mage trails off while clawing at his throat.

"What's happening?" I take a step only to stop when I sway on my feet, my hand latching onto Zoltan's forearm to steady myself.

The mage gasps and slumps on the wall, sweat rolling down his purpled face in rivulets as he gulps air.

"He can't speak of what he knows." Zoltan turns to me, all the aloofness on his face disappearing when he sees the blood gushing from my side. "You are hurt."

"I'm fine." I hiss through my teeth when he scoops me in his arms. "He needs to spill what he knows."

"He will." Zoltan rushes through the broken door like the Titans themselves are on his heels. "Trust me love, he will."

What in the worlds can scare the Daywalker so much?

"Oh, dear fates, I'm dying." My panicked whisper is the last thing I say before darkness swallows me whole.

Chapter Thirteen

I have no idea how I could possibly be on a boat but the surface underneath me keeps swaying, the movements sloshing the contents of my stomach to the point that I feel like I'm about to puke. With a groan, I turn on my side in case it really happens, and half of my face sinks into a soft pillow, which blocks my nostrils along with my ability to breathe.

"I've never been a big believer in the fates, but you are changing my beliefs, Drake."

Popping one eye open I find Leo watching me from a few feet away, his face flipped sideways from my position on the bed. Not a boat then, just my head swimming from something. Did I end up with the mother of all hangovers because I drank too much last night? Everything is fuzzy after spending many hours on Zoltan's bed.

A spike of adrenaline jolts my heart into a gallop, but I calm instantly. There is no way Zoltan spiraled out of control and took too much blood. It could explain why I'm feeling like this, yet, all the way to my core I know it's not true. When exactly I started trusting him so much is beyond me, and definitely not something I'm willing to look into right now.

"Where am I?" Croaking, I wet my dry lips, my throat sore like I've been chewing glass for dinner.

"Don't talk." Leo jumps from the chair he occupies, disappearing from my line of sight. "Here. Drink this." Reappearing next to me, the bed dips right before his hand lift my head.

Keeping an eye on the alpha from my periphery, I greedily gulp the glass of water he holds to my lips. The icy liquid feels like it's tearing my insides apart as it goes down, and when I drain the last drop, I suck in air as if I can't get enough.

"What in all hells happened?" Each word is followed by a pathetic gasp.

"The fates." Leo growls, his face twisting in a grimace like he can't believe he is saying it.

I gape at him.

"What?"

"You don't remember what happened last night?" The skepticism dripping from each syllable pisses me off.

"Of course I do, pup. I just love lying to you." Flipping the covers off me in frustration, I yank them to my chin the same second. "Where the fuck are my clothes?" Craning my neck, I glance around for the first time, a pained groan escaping my chest when the floor and ceiling switch places and everything around me spins. "Where am I?" Not even pressing a hand to my forehead stops the room from swaying.

When the alpha says nothing, I glare at him. "It smells like you. How did I get here?" The first scents drift through my nostrils, or maybe my brain is finally getting online and registering them. Whatever it may be, I have no doubt this is Leo's room.

And you are naked in his bed, my inner bitch drawls unhelpfully.

"You couldn't resist not knowing, so you had to check the goods yourself, Drake." Leo smirks, wiggling his eyebrows at me.

"You mean you had to totally knock me out to drag my unconscious body here." Glowering at him, I almost miss the searching look in his eyes. Like he is waiting on me to say something. Or remember. He's debating whether he should say anything or not. The struggle is visible on his handsome face, so I decide to help him out. "Start talking."

"Whoa, I like this bossy side of you." Leo's voice is teasing and light, but I see his wolf lurking behind the green irises and he isn't pleased at the idea of anyone trying to dominate him.

At my unimpressed look, the alpha sighs and his shoulders slump. Preoccupied with my hangover and my lack of clothing, I didn't realize how stiff he was, the lines at the corners of his mouth etched deeper into his tanned skin.

"You really don't remember?" All humor gone, Leo gives my thigh a comforting squeeze. My heart drops to my stomach. I'm unable to speak, so I just shake my head. "You and Zoltan stopped an assassination attempt on the mage Board member. Daren's father," he adds as if I've seriously lost my mind and need reminding of that little twist.

The events of the night come back like a bucket of cold water over my head, chilling me to the marrow of my bones. Keeping the cover clutched between my breasts, I flick the side to find my ribs covered with unblemished skin. The same place the hunter stabbed me, twisting his dagger until blood gushed out of a hole the size of my fist. I should feel dizzy thinking about it, or at least relieved because I'm healed and very much alive. Instead, a new wave of fury rushes through my veins. I almost got myself killed to protect the old fucker when I should have been leaving him to whatever the fates had in store for him.

"How long was I out?"

"Almost sixty-eight hours."

"My mother?" as much as I hate to worry about her, I really don't want her dead.

"As soon as Zoltan roared through the hallways with you bleeding in his arms, Astara took her back to Sienna until we figure out what's going on." Leo is fast to assure me. I'm trying hard not to think of having a worried look plastered on my face. Nope, that's not me. She can take care of herself.

"Zoltan healed me?" Deciding to push those thought aside for now, I refocus on Leo. "Where is he? And why in the worlds did he bring me here?"

"He was looking for Daren." His green gaze flicks between mine. "Your friend saved your life in more ways than one last night. Again."

"What are you talking about? Can you not be like the rest of them?" Snapping at him, I take a deep breath. I remind myself internally as I wrestle my anger into submission. "Let's use simple words, pup, not riddles. My head feels like it's going to explode." The jab I always throw his way has his bulging arm muscles relaxing.

"The dagger the hunter used was meant for a powerful mage, Drake." The color drains slightly from Leo's face. "It was coated with something that drains magic when it comes in contact with blood. Out of all the unfortunate events you've had the last few days, having Daren's blood in you actually saved your life."

I don't know what to say so I just stare at him mute, my knuckles white where I'm strangling the sheets.

"If it wasn't for his magic running through you, Fenrir said it would've started draining your dragon blood powers. Neither him nor Zoltan could stop the bleeding. Daren stepped in and fed you his life force until they were able to find Myst, and then she closed the wound." Leo's Adam's apple bobs up and down when he swallows thickly. "I've never seen anything like it in my life."

"You've never seen anything like what Myst did?" The words are a whisper through my numbs lips, the gravity of the situation hitting home like a sledgehammer to the back of my skull.

"No." A lock of hair falls over his forehead as he shakes his head jerkily. "What Daren did, Drake." Another thick swallow follows, the hairs on his forearms lifting as if static is pulling them off his skin. "The male gave you so much blood he barely had a heartbeat. I have sworn to protect you. I'd like to think you call me a friend, but I'm ashamed to say I'm not sure I would've done the same thing. Dying to protect you in a battle? Any fucking day. Sitting calmly with determination while you drink me dry? No fucking way."

Leo shudders.

I shudder, too.

"Where is Daren now?" I sound choked up, a lump the size of a fist clogging my throat.

"Fenrir and Myst did something to help him sleep and heal." With a shuddering sigh, the alpha scrubs a hand over his face. He looks so tired my heart clenches at the sight. "He is okay, thank fuck. Both of you are okay." Muttering more to himself than me, he rubs the top of his head and makes his thick hair stick out in every direction.

"What were those things?" my spine rattles from the

tremor raking it. "That shifter looked mutated and sick." The half transformed furry body will haunt my dreams for years to come.

"Zoltan thinks is a result with the blood Roberti is manipulating. He said the creature was adamant to reach the mage. Its entire focus was on the Board member even when fighting a vampire like Zoltan." A line forms between Leo's eyebrows, his gaze losing focus. I can only imagine how disturbing the news is to the alpha. Seeing the mutated creature messed me up, as well. I've delayed things enough, but since none of us can figure out what exactly is going on, I think I owe an ancient Fae a visit.

For a wakeup call.

Jumping off the bed, I have to grab onto the mattress so I don't face plant on the floor. The room flips upside down, but it rights itself fast enough that before Leo realizes what I'm about to do, I'm already rummaging through his drawers. Fuck nudity. I need clothes. There is fire churning in the pit of my stomach, spreading through my limbs. Pulling out what looks like a pair of boxer briefs and a tank top, I yank them over my body and almost topple over in my haste.

"Zoltan said not to let you out of bed." The alpha stands in the middle of the room with his arms crossed over broad chest, all the weariness disappearing as he blocks my exit.

"Where is Zoltan?" Twisting the waistband of the briefs, I tie a knot so I don't end up wearing them around my ankles.

"He had words to say to the Board." Narrowing his eyes on me, Leo shifts to the balls of his feet, ready to pounce if I bolt for the door. "I won't be surprised if he nails them in the foyer for all to see. He was livid when he stormed out of here."

"You really think you're going to stop me from leaving this room." Barking out a laugh, I tilt my head at him. "How cute."

"I watched you die and come back too many times over too many hours, Drake." A deep, feral growl comes out of his chest, raising the hairs on the back of my neck. "You want to leave? You'll have to knock me out first." The green of his eyes flickers, the intelligent animal residing inside him coming to play, too. "Where do you think you'll be going?"

I can fight him. My head is still filled with cotton, there is a distant buzzing in my ears, and my legs feel like they are made out of jelly, but the dragon blood power is churning like simmering lava waiting to burst and turn everything to ashes, albeit sluggishly. Judging by the doubling size of Leo's shoulders, I'll lose, too, because the shifter is eager to prove that he can go neck and neck with a freak like me.

Or I can tell him the truth. He will either agree it's the smartest thing to do or we will brawl anyway. Only because I really need to get out of here, I opt to play it smart, so I slap my hands on my hips and look down my nose at him. Channeling Fenrir might work in my favor.

"I'm going to see Soren." His lips part but I stab the air, my finger pointing right at his nose. "Don't you dare lecture me. There is no way we are going to keep putting ourselves into the line of fire and getting hurt while the asshole takes a nap. This should matter to him as much as us, if not more. I'm waking his ass up if it's the last thing I do. Now, get out of my way."

"That is a very bad idea, Drake," he hisses through clenched teeth, but I see doubt flickering in his gaze. "Soren might have a soft spot for you, but he is not a harmless creature you can boss around. You'll regret this sooner than you think."

"I do not boss anyone around." The incredulity on Leo's face makes my palm itch to slap him. "Get out of my way."

"Let's wait for Zoltan and Fenrir to come back, yes?" Changing tactics to make it appear as if he is on my side and wants to help, the alpha even flashes me his trademark cocky grin. "If all of them agree that you should attempt waking the Fae, you'll do it then. Trust me on this, Soren awake will not be what you expect. I'm not old enough to speak from experience but the stories I've heard? If half of them are true, we will have more problems than help with him walking the grounds."

Uneasiness is digging a hole in my stomach but not enough to change my mind. Whatever kind of asshole Soren is, I know in my gut he will not go around killing people because he is greedy for power. *That's because there is no one around more powerful than him,* a small voice whispers through my mind but it's too faint to change the course of my plan. No, this is the right move. What's the worst thing that can happen? The old Fae won't want to get involved? Well, that is no different than before, then. And if he does decide to help, then at least I can ask him for advice. Plus, those three old fucks are terrified of him, which means he can be their own personal boogeyman. With him near, we will have no problem keeping their asses in control. And after Roberti is dealt with, I'll kill them all. I tell Leo as much.

"It sounds like a great plan, but in my experience, everything that sounds simple never works out as you expect it. In the situation we are in"—Leo rolls his shoulders, relaxing his stance for the first time since I jumped out of the bed, while all my muscles coil up——"simple is stupid. Simple can get us all killed."

"You are right." His head jerks back like he got punched, eyes widening comically. "Simple is stupid."

Not giving him time to react, I jump and spin, my foot connecting with the center of his chest. Leo is not expecting it, and all the air rushes out of his lungs on a groan. He flies back and hits the headboard of his bed, the wooden structure cracking under his weight. Stumbling forward as my head spins like crazy, I dash for the door and yank it open with enough force to rip it off the top hinges, the wood tilting to the side and the edge jabbing me in the head—like I need something else to make the damn thing have its own heartbeat.

"Drake!" Leo's outraged roar propels my feet faster than if hunters were on my heels.

With my arms pumping, my head spinning, and bile rising to the back of my throat, I sprint through the building until the familiar golden hallway comes into view. The alpha is chasing me. I can feel my shoulder blades prickling from his furious gaze. As soon as I step foot behind the invisible barrier, no one can stop me from waking Soren up. The soles of my feet barely skim the ground.

I wish Leo's warnings were not playing on repeat in my head.

Chapter Fourteen

My hand poised above the door ready to knock, I hesitate.

I've never knocked before when coming to see the old Fae, so why start now? All the previous times I was in a rush or not thinking clearly, usually allowing my emotions to guide my actions. Not that standing here right now is any different. I'm here acting on impulse … again.

"Damn Leo and his stupid warnings." Huffing under my breath I curl my fingers around the doorknob and yank it open.

My feet falter for just a second before I step through the threshold, the scent of crushed pine and restless waters washing over me and calming my racing heart. Soren is always surrounded by potent air that is filled with a sense of peace and an edge of danger. It confuses the senses for sure, more like a siren song luring one closer even only for that person to end up dead.

"You are being an idiot right now, Franky." Muttering to myself, I close the door behind me with a soft click, leaning back on it while my eyes dart around the room.

It's exactly the same as always. The humongous bed takes up most of the space, while Soren's body is like a lump covered with the silky sheets in the center of it all, unmoving. Golden, glittery accents sparkle throughout, reflecting the moonlight peeking through the pulled-apart curtains on the wall-to-ceiling windows, their frames of carved wood resembling twisted roots of ancient trees. What I've failed to notice before are the jewels imbedded in every available space, like eyes of some lurking beasts waiting for their next prey.

A shiver slithers up and down my spine lifting the short hairs on my arms.

Like a punch to the gut, a feeling of anger and worry spreads through my bond with Zoltan, jolting me upright. Of course, the alpha ran straight to the Daywalker to tattle on me. That means I don't have much time. The vampire might not be able to cross the wards protecting Soren's wing of the academy, but that doesn't mean there won't be hells to pay when I do get out of here. The thought gives me pause, but it's not enough to change my mind.

"What's he going to do when I show up with Soren on my heels? Ground me?" Snickering uneasily, I inch closer to the large bed.

Soren's face is too beautiful a face for any mortal eyes, and like some creep, I loom over him while he sleeps. Chewing on the inside of my mouth, I search his features for any indication that he is aware I'm invading his personal space. Nothing. Not even a flutter of his thick eyelashes or a change in his breathing.

I frown.

Should I be insulted that he doesn't perceive me as a threat? Or maybe I should be honored that the Fae has so much trust in me? Either way, he knows I'm here. He would never allow anyone in his rooms without knowing. *He might be long gone out of his mind, Franky. Maybe he wishes for death and hopes you'll end his life.* My breath picks up at the thought. *If Soren dies, you are fucked. You'll be the only life feeding the magic of this place, you dumbass,* another voice snaps in my head. My spine stiffens.

"You tricky, tricky, Fae." I breathe the words as I step close enough that my thighs bump the mattress. "It's not that you trust me. You just know I'm not stupid enough to screw myself up like that."

Not even the twitch of a muscle on Soren's face.

"Time to wake up, sleeping beauty." Crawling on top of the bed on my knees, I lean over him, my heartbeat thundering in my ears. "If you don't open your eyes, I'm not waking you up with a kiss. It will be a punch to your nose."

Silver hair slides over the pillow from the bed dipping under my weight, Soren's body shifts closer to me when the mattress gives under me. A slight spike in the charged air is all I get as an answer to my threat. Placing my hands on either side of his head, my elbows bend until our noses are almost touching.

"You will talk to me, Soren. The time for ignoring everything that is happening here is long gone. The lives of everyone in this place are more *your* responsibility than mine." The soft breath wafting from his nostrils tickles my lips. "I promised you I'd dress you in a pink tutu last time, but I think I'll drag your unconscious ass butt naked in the middle of the foyer if I have to. Now, wake up!"

Nothing.

Fear that he might truly not wake up mixes with anger from the blatant way he ignores everything here. All the people dying while he sleeps. All those I've come to care about fighting for their lives while he does nothing. Is this damn brick and mortar building and the piece of land it sits on really all he cares about? Does that matter to him more than any life, including my own? The monstrosity living inside me perks up at those thoughts, sending a sharp pulse of magic through my veins, my skin prickling like I've touched a live wire. Colors come alive around me, Soren's face gaining an ethereal glow like an apparition laying in front of my eyes. I feel my dragon blood coming to the surface, stretching my skin to the point of pain to accommodate us both.

"Dùisg seann dràgon, marbhaidh mi thu nad chadal." The foreign words purr from my lips, the back of my skull numbing from the threat in them even when I don't understand what I just said.

Soren's lips twitch at the corners, the relief that I finally got a reaction buckling my arms enough that my nose bumps into his. His eyes snap open stopping my heart in my chest before it kicks into overdrive and hammers my ribs. *Oh shit, oh shit,* my mind screams on repeat, but I'm frozen like deer in headlights lost in his gaze. Golden irises seer into me, the vertical pupils expanding and retracting on my face. With a very embarrassing squeak, I shove away from him and fall on my ass, crab crawling backward until I reach the edge of the bed.

"Gealladh dàna de dhragon òg, fear nach urrainn dhut a chumail suas." The husky, deep quality of his voice caresses my insides, turning my bones to mush, while something in the back of my mind is shrieking that I'll die here if I don't get my ass away from him.

Soren sits up, his movements fluid and hypnotizing like a cobra coming out of a basket ready to strike. The covers pool around his waist lodging the harsh breaths in my throat when the full expanse of his naked torso come into view.

Holy fuck. I'm surrounded daily by supernaturals that are created to be perfect in every way to lure their pray. Zoltan himself kicks my heart into overdrive with his physical presence, even when he is dressed. Nothing can prepare a person for Soren, though. Gods and angels will weep seeing his face. Long silver hair like a waterfall glides over his wide shoulders and chest, every muscle chiseled to perfection, the tips of his pointed ears peeking through the strands. The moonlight creates shadows over all the dips and bumps of his abdominals, the smooth skin making my hands itch to touch him, and like a moron, my mouth waters at the viral male in front of me. Judging by the amused look on his face, he knows it too.

Jerk!

"What?" Yes, I know, very intelligent come back. The corner of his full lips tilting up tells me I *am* an idiot.

"You still do not understand your dragon, Francesca." Soren is unnaturally still and it unnerves me to no end.

"I was a little busy staying alive. No time for language lessons." Familiar anger bursts through me shaking off the stupefied state I'm in. "Care to share, old male?

The soft chuckle flipflops my stomach. I glare at him.

"Ah"—He sighs, stretching his arms over his head, and I swipe the back of my hand over my mouth in case of any drool— "the beauty of being so young. Young and foolish." A dangerous glint enters his gaze, and it lifts the hairs on the back of my neck.

"If wanting to stop power-hungry monsters from killing us all is 'foolish' then by all means, old one, I'm the biggest fool there is." If I keep glaring so hard, I fear my face will permanently freeze like this.

"This again." Leaning back on his arms, he cocks his head. "We spoke about power and those that always hunger for it, child. Was I not clear enough?" The fact that he looks like we are the same age but calls me a child is not lost on me. It's weird as fuck.

"Roberti is manipulating blood and creating an army in the human realm." His eyebrows jerk up when I blurt that out. "They are hunting half-bloods and using them, or so we think." And because I'm an idiot, I can't stop talking. "I killed my brother."

This last part gets more interest than the mention of a mutant army from Soren. "Another Dragon Blood?"

"No." I frown at him. "Different father but half-blood none the less." When he keeps staring at me, I get frustrated. "Didn't you hear that I killed him? Me. I was holding the blade that separated his head from his shoulders. At my initiation," I add the last part through a clenched jaw.

"I wondered if they'd brave that." Nodding thoughtfully, he swings his legs on the side of the bed.

My heart stops.

I will go to my grave without admitting to anyone, including myself, that I am greatly disappointed when he stands up to reveal the silky pants covering his lower half. Sitting low on his narrow hips, they don't hide the corded muscle of his lower body, nor the pert ass and powerful thighs they are veiling from me. Thankfully, he is looking around and doesn't see me checking him out. I don't care if he sees me, though. One would have to be dead not to look. Upon further thought, that's debatable too. I'm almost certain he would probably raise a dead person.

"What did I say to wake you?" Needing a distraction, I busy myself with jumping off the bed.

"You told me if I don't wake up, you'll kill me asleep." Soren grins, flashing his straight white teeth like he's the star of a toothpaste commercial. "I told you not to promise something you cannot endure." Cocking his head to the side, his smile grows. "I am willing to test it, Francesca. Are you?"

"I've threatened you before," I point out as I step away from him, which only adds to his amusement. "It never worked until now."

"You have, yes." Soren prowls close to me, ignoring my personal bubble just like I did earlier in my attempt to get a reaction from him. I hold my breath. "But never your dragon, Francesca. She called to me because she needs me. She is a prideful little thing, and she's been hiding until now. I will never ignore her call, so here I am."

"Gee thanks. You haven't lost your mind, have you? You do know 'her' life is my life. I've asked for help before, so I wish I knew speaking in tongues would do the trick." Turning to step away from him, my body locks when he tucks a strand of hair behind my ear.

"She is strong enough to protect you, never doubt that." His hand lingers close to my face for a long moment before he flicks it nonchalantly. "The others can fend for themselves."

"You will help, right?" Ignoring his last comment because it sours the taste in my mouth, I peer at him hopefully as Leo's warnings come to the front of my mind. "We have to stop them before they build that army, if it's not too late already, and before they release any of the Titans."

"No one can release the Titians." Thank fuck he steps away so I can breathe. "The book is protected, I made sure of that."

"The book they actually managed to steal? The same one we recovered while you were having a nap, you mean?" His head jerks in my direction and his hair flies like a flag around it. "Someone hasn't been paying very close attention, has he?"

"They bypassed the wards." It's not a question so I don't answer. "Very well, young one. Let us see what they've been doing while I keep them all alive and at peak strength."

My feet stay rooted to the spot when Soren spins on his heel and heads for the door. The globe of his ass makes waves appear on his silky pants, and the muscles of his broad back bunch and twist with his movements. His toes peek from the loose bottoms as he pads over the thick rugs covering the floor of his rooms, the silent steps as unnerving as the predatory way his body moves. He pauses when he realizes I'm not following him.

Throwing a look over his shoulder, he says, "Are we not going?" He turns to face me and I swallow to wet my dry mouth. "Was there something else you wanted to speak to me about alone?" Fear stabs me at the back of my head when I see an expectant glint in those golden eyes.

There is eagerness there like he can barely contain himself at the idea of hearing words coming out of my mouth. What those words are I have no idea, but I know deep in my soul I never want to say them out loud. Blinking fast, I clear the cobwebs clouding my head.

"You are not putting clothes on?" My hand jerks up and down, indicating his half-naked appearance. "A shirt at least." My eyes drop to the silky pants and I gulp at the tenting at his groin. "And pants. Yup, definitely pants. Thick fabric preferably. It gets chilly outside."

With a groan, I snap my mouth shut and ignore the mirth dancing on his face the longer.

"I make you uncomfortable." He does not sound worried at all. Actually, he sounds excited.

"What?" I take a step back when he moves closer. "No!

I'm thinking about you." And every other person who is alive with hormones that will see you like this. "You want to blend in, you know."

"It does not bother you when I am like this?" His hand moves over his chest to his abdominals, pulling my gaze with it like I'm under a spell.

I jerk it back up to his face with a glower. "No, I couldn't care less."

"Then let us go." Before I think of anything else to say, he is already out the door.

"Fuck." Rubbing a hand over my face harshly, I blow out a breath. "Maybe I should've listened to Leo."

Soren's laugh from down the hallway spurs me on, and I rush to catch up with him.

This will be another clusterfuck. I can feel it.

Chapter Fifteen

Seeing the welcoming party at the end of the golden hallway with their gloomy faces makes me want to turn around and go hide in Soren's rooms. The Fae in question is one step behind me, walking close enough that I can feel the heat from his body burning my skin and his hand bumping my hip as it swings with each step. Zoltan's glare follows Soren's hand like he's tracking prey he plans on killing as soon as it's within reach. Soren's soft chuckle tells me he is well aware of that, too, though it's clear he doesn't give a shit. Jerk.

"You don't have to walk close enough to trip me." Snarling at Soren without moving my lips, I jut my chin out. No way I'll cower in front of Zoltan.

"Where will be the fun in that, Francesca?"

"Asshole."

Soren laughs out loud and I look at him over my shoulder. Big mistake. His head is thrown back, his whole face lighting up as if I just told him something that makes him happy. My heart shrivels in my chest, and when I see Zoltan again, I realize the Fae is playing a very dangerous game. If thunder had a face, it would look exactly like the vampire right now.

My feet move faster, and I don't care that I'm actually speed walking away from Soren. Fenrir, Leo, and Daren squirm behind Zoltan as if itching to bolt and meet me half way. *It's fine,* I lie to myself. *Soren will help me get rid of Roberti and then he can go back to sleep.* I don't even believe my own words. Something nags at my mind, telling me I should've left the Fae alone, but it's too late now.

As soon as my foot is out of the hallway, Zoltan snatches my arm and yanks me against him. With an oomph, I grab his shoulders, startled by the strength of his hold, but he is not even looking at me. His thunderous glare is trained over my shoulder at the jerk chuckling merrily behind me.

"Zoltan," Soren says, humor evident in his words. "It has been a long time."

"Not long enough it seems." The vampire growls, his chest thrumming from the depth of his voice.

"Soren." Fenrir folds his body in a bow, his nose almost touching the floor. My eyebrows crawl all the way to my hairline. "It is an honor to have you among us."

"Is it, young royal?" The underlying bite in his words stiffens my spine. "You wished for me not to wake and see your failure."

"We all failed." Wiggling like I'm crazy, I turn in Zoltan's arms, which are squeezing me like metal shackles, to face Soren. "Why are you blaming Fenrir? You slept through it all, in case you have forgotten."

They all ignore me, Soren and Fenrir locked in a staring match. Power whirls around us, stealing my breath, and whatever air exits my lungs clouds in front of my face. The temperature in the building drops to freezing levels, making my teeth chatter. No one else reacts to it, every male coiled as if they'll start fighting every second. My eyes dart around and I notice sparks sputtering from Daren's fingers, while Leo's body grows in size as he readies himself to shift. Well fuck, not exactly what I was expecting when bringing Soren to join us.

"Why are we ..." my voice trails off when a mind-numbing cry echoes off the walls and Tenebris jumps between the two Fae.

The black fur along his spine is standing on end, his front paws bent and his head lowered with both ears pinned. He's ready to pounce on Soren if he dares move an inch. The thick tail is lashing in agitation behind him, and a low growl vibrates from his chest on a never-ending rumble. It's enough to break the stare Soren had on Fenrir, and the freezing air automatically disappears.

"Tenebris?" Soren blinks at the shifter as if coming out of a daze.

The panther snarls.

Zoltan does, too.

"Can we take this somewhere else?" Breaking out of my own riled-up state, I hiss at them. "As soon as the Board hears Soren is awake, they'll be on our assess."

Glancing around proves my point. People are gaping at us, some pale and ready to faint, while others are awed as if they're about to drop on their knees and start worshiping the old Fae. Old in age, not in appearance. *They'll all worship him if they pull those silky pants down, that's for sure.* My mind is still stuck in the gutter and it is not helping at all.

"Very wise, young dragon." Soren smiles at me like he's indulging a child. "Let us move out of sight, shall we?"

He is the first to take a step, his long legs in those damn pants eating the space with purpose. The rest of the males move in sync behind him like they're guarding a dangerous prisoner, Zoltan leaving me behind like he wasn't just trying to break my ribcage with his arms a second ago. Left behind, I gawk at all of them as they move further down the halls.

"Well, I'll be damned," Astara breathes, materializing next to me. "Holy shit, Franky." She audibly swallows, and I turn to the side to see her better before following the direction of her gaze.

"Yeah." An incredulous snicker that holds anything but humor bursts out of me when I see her checking out Soren's ass.

"This will be a problem." Linking her arm through mine, she drags me behind the males, who are marching in front of us with purpose. At least she doesn't remember she's supposed to be upset with me.

"You think?" My drawl doesn't go unanswered.

"Don't get me wrong, I'm livid that you went to Myst instead of me. But holy shit, this makes up for a sliver of it." Tinkling laughter makes her shoulders shake. "This will drive my brother insane." The blue gaze matching Zoltan's pins me intently. "I don't envy you right now."

"You are drooling as well, in case you didn't notice. You'll get shit about it, too." To prove my point, I lift her unhinged jaw to close her mouth.

"Yes, but unlike you I can also touch. It'll be worth the tongue lashing. Speaking of tongues ..." Her whole body shivers and her face lights with a hungry grin. Snickering with glee, her eyes sparkle. "Don't worry, I'll tell you all the details. Every inch of it, because I'm a good friend like that."

I have no time to reply before she is gone, practically running after Soren. Not knowing if I should laugh or cry given the situation, I drag my feet behind all of them, following at a safe distance. If I think Zoltan has forgotten all about me, I am sorely mistaken. That too-blue gaze keeps track of me as much as it does Soren. With the stand-off between the Fae, the lectures I'm going to get are only delayed. If I'm lucky, though, it'll be a while before Zoltan gives me a piece of his mind.

Dread gnaws at my gut when I see them entering the dining hall. Which part of staying out of sight didn't they get? This is the same as going to the Board and screaming, "Hey, look, Soren is awake." Memories assault my brain, everything in front of my eyes swimming in blood, my brother's head rolling over the metal bed and hitting the floor with a dull thud, and a squelching sound. Cold sweat drenches my shirt and I rub my sweaty palms on the fabric of Leo's briefs.

Oh shit. I forgot that on top of everything else, I'm dressed in the alpha's clothing. No wonder Zoltan is acting insane. I won't be surprised if he actually locks me in a cage later so I can't get the scent of another male on me. First was Daren's blood, which he didn't mention since it saved my life after the explosion. Then it happened again after the dagger carved me up while saving the old fart. Now dressed in the shifter's undergarments with a half-naked Fae at my back. Vampires are possessive as hell. Zoltan's control is truly admirable. *Or he will really lock you up later,* my mind supplies unhelpfully. It serves me good thinking about it, otherwise I may not even enter the cursed dining hall.

A ripple passes over my body as I step inside. Frowning, my gaze moves around taking notice of the lack of tables and furniture and the pristine walls and floor without a trace of blood in sight. All evidence of the murder I committed has been erased from existence like it never happened, wiping away the existence of my brother along with it. Life his life never mattered to any of them. *It didn't.* The voice in my head makes the fury I pushed aside bubble to the surface.

"Fenrir covered it up with his gift." Zoltan's deep voice pulls me out of my churning thoughts. I didn't even notice him coming to stand next to me. "I didn't think you'd want to see blood covering everything."

"It's still there?" Hands fisting to my sides, I narrow my eyes and attempt to see through the illusion. "Am I standing in his blood right now?" Bile burns the back of my throat.

Zoltan pries my fingers open, lacing his through them to stop me from digging the nails into the skin of my palms. Lifting the back of my hand to his lips, he presses a kiss on it and tugs me closer. My nostrils flare, but apart from his sinful scent, nothing else fills my lungs.

"He is protecting it from being disturbed, too," he murmurs in my ear, his mouth grazing the skin. "We need to test every drop spilled here before it's cleaned up. Besides, I wouldn't let anyone touch anything before you are ready to part with him, Francesca. You have my word."

Pushing down the lump choking me, I look up at him. "Thank you." The intensity of his gaze drags me under, and I lose myself for a second in the all-consuming presence that is Zoltan. "You are not angry with me?" Leaning closer to him, my body molds to him like the missing piece of a puzzle.

"Oh, I am livid." Fire flashes through his irises and jolts me out of the daze. "But not at you, Love." Pressing his forehead to mine, he sighs. "Never at you."

"As touching as this is, I believe I was brought here for a reason," Soren calls out, breaking the bubble surrounding me in all that is Zoltan.

"Right." Snorting ungracefully, I step out of the vampire's embrace. "We wouldn't want to keep you waiting, you sleeping jerk."

A couple of sofas and a few chairs sit in the corner of the large room. I'm not sure if they were there when I walked in or if Fenrir conjured them out of thin air. The more I learn about the Fae's powers, the more confusing it gets. So, I don't try to understand it because it'll end up driving me crazy.

"I told him about the manipulation of blood Roberti is doing, as well as the book." Deciding to just go for it, I stride to the closest chair and plop on it. "He was living under the impression that his wards can't be broken."

"They can't." Folding his arms over his naked chest, Soren cocks his chin up.

Astara sighs … loudly.

I choke mine down, thank fuck.

"Yet, I have the book in my possession after they almost took it in the human realm." Zoltan glares at his sister, lowering himself on the armrest of my chair.

"Have they used her blood to break through the wards?" The arrogance drains from the ancient Fae, replaced with tightening creases around his freakish eyes and mouth.

"They did get some of my blood from the few fights we've had in the human realm." I look around the faces of my friends and search for confirmation that I'm right. Hoping for it, actually. "But not enough to do everything they've succeeded in doing. Right?"

Fenrir is first to assure me. "No, Hellion. They will need more than that to neutralize the wards as well."

"There is a serious problem then." Soren moves around me, bumping my knees on purpose as he passes me, I'm sure. Lowering himself on the closest sofa, he throws an arm behind him, hugging the back of it. "Last time I opened those wards to check on the book was … ten years ago?" His head tilts to the side, his gaze going unfocused. "Maybe fifteen?"

The blood drains from my head, my ears buzzing with white noise thundering like a freight train through my skull.

"Drake?" Leo's frantic shout makes me jump out of my skin.

"Around the time Roberti took me under the agency to work for him." I swallow the panic down.

"He didn't know what you were at the time." Zoltan points out, but he is as stiff as a rock next to me, not believing his own statement.

"That we know of. He might've hoped." Looking at Zoltan's face, I dig my nails in the cushion of the chair. "He is always playing the long game, never forget that."

"Who knew that you were checking the wards, Soren?" Zoltan is fuming, while Soren looks like we are talking about the weather.

"The rest of the Board, of course." The ancient Fae arches an eyebrow like the vampire is asking a stupid question.

"I was right, then. They are helping Roberti." Snarling the words, I want to scream in frustration.

"Bring the three of them to me."

All the hairs on my body stand up at the promise of death in Soren's words.

Chapter Sixteen

"You shouldn't be snoop … investigating," Zoltan whispers in my ear. He chooses smart words, but he scares the shit out of me in the process.

Elbowing him doesn't do shit, so I push and shove on his shoulders until he gets his ass moving. We need to get away from the door that, until he decided to come and interrupt me, I had my ear pressed against. His shoulders are shaking with suppressed laughter, but even though it's pissing me off, he at least saunters away before they hear the commotion. *Look on the bright side, Franky.*

"Bright side, my ass." Muttering to myself, I keep a fistful of his shirt so he doesn't get away.

"I find it adorable when you do that, Love." My heart skips a beat when he looks at me with half-closed eyelids, hunger burning in his gaze.

"Why are you here?" Opting not to take the bait, I shove harder, releasing his shirt when we are far enough from the double doors that Soren closed in our face more than an hour ago. "You can't tell me you are not curious what's being said in there." Stabbing a finger behind me, pain spreads through my shoulder from the sharp move.

"You want to tell me that you woke up the most powerful being alive and you don't trust him?" Zoltan might tell me he is not angry with me, but the mocking way his eyebrow cocks as he narrows his eyes at me says otherwise.

"Do you?" Mimicking his stance, I try not to fidget. He does have a good point, not that I'll tell him that.

"I did not bring Soren into the situation we find ourselves, Love." That makes my feet shuffle slightly. "According to Leo, you were quite adamant to wake him up. So, here we are."

After demanding the Board to be brought to him, Soren listened with rapt attention to the recap of everything that has happened so far. Occasionally, he flicked angry looks Fenrir's way, especially when going over the part when Zoltan was taken and found feral. I didn't like the calculating look on the ancient Fae's face at all, or the side-eyed glances he kept throwing my way after that. When I asked what it was that Fenrir failed to do, I was ignored like I hadn't spoken, which irked me to no end. The cherry on top of the cake was Soren cupping my face tenderly as he told me to stay behind with the rest and he would find me after he was done with the Board. It wasn't only Zoltan snarling at his touch, but me as well. I don't understand what game the Fae is playing, but I'm not going to be a willing participant.

"The Board is working with Roberti. We need him or more lives will be lost." If I keep repeating it, it'll be true.

Zoltan sighs, all the fight from a second ago draining out of him in a wave. "We could've gone from a different angle, but what's done, is done." Taking my hand, he tugs gently and I fall in step with him. "Let's find the others. It will not be wise for Soren to find you here."

"You make it sound like he will hurt me." My snort dies a sudden death at the somber look on his face. "You can't be serious."

"With beings as ancient as him, it's hard to tell when something will provoke them." I can tell it costs him to stay calm and not yell at me. It's physically obvious by his clenched jaw and the muscle ticking there with its own heartbeat. "Soren is indulging you, more than I thought possible, if I am honest." That last part sounds like it's said more for himself than me. "You will be wise to stay on your toes around him."

"You sound more like a jealous lover than an advisor for my wellbeing."

"I am both." My heart skips a beat at the smoldering gaze locked on my face. "Mark my words, Love. I will not give you up, to Roberti, to this damn place, or to Soren. I will burn this realm down before allowing anyone to sever the bond between us. You will be smart to take this as the truth it is. From now on, everything that happens is in your hands."

"Wow, gloomy much?" A nervous chuckle bubbles from my numb lips. "It's beyond even your normal brooding self. No, wait! How would you say it again?" Tapping a finger on my chin, I give him a once over. "Right. It doesn't become you, Zoltan."

He doesn't laugh.

Nor does he react in any way apart from watching me with no expression on his handsome face. We are all on edge thanks to the psychos trying to kill us, which must be why Zoltan is giving me all these creepy scenarios. I disobeyed him and didn't stay where he told me to, so now he is messing with my mind. It must be that. The fact he can manipulate my brain but doesn't is something I choose to ignore. I never said I was smart, just that I'm good at surviving … somehow.

"Duly noted." Leaning heavily on his arm, I stare at my feet so he doesn't see my face burning red. "You have nothing to worry about, bloodsucker. You've ruined me for any other male, ancient or otherwise."

Zoltan's finger crooks under my chin as he lifts my face to his. Those blue eyes burning through mine sear me all the way to my soul. "Swear that it is the truth."

"Why are you being obnoxious right now?" Huffing, I try to jerk my head away but he doesn't let me. "You know it's true, you asshole." I glare at him when he locks my head between his hands and holds me prisoner.

"Swear it."

"I swear it." Pushing the words through clenched teeth, I gasp when he slams his mouth on mine, his tongue diving in and stealing my senses with it.

My hands grab his shoulders and I claw at him to bring him closer. His overwhelming scent fills my lungs and my knees buckle. Zoltan's arms wrap around me and hold me upright. His breath becomes mine and I can feel him every-where. The bond between us feeds me, but hunger for this vampire has reached unbearable levels. I can't tell if it's his need or mine, and in this moment, I don't really care. Zoltan sings through my veins, branding the blood that is pumping like crazy under my skin.

The clearing of a throat brings my brain online, but Zoltan doesn't move. Leisurely, he glides his tongue around mine before releasing it, his lips lingering over mine for a long moment. The twitch of his mouth betrays him. The jerk did this on purpose because he knew someone was coming. Keeping my forehead pressed on his because my legs are too wobbly to move away, I look to the side. Soren is watching us with way too much interest.

"How did it go?" Much to Zoltan's amusement, I have to clear my throat twice to speak.

"They are hiding something." Soren walks straight at us, physically separating the vampire from me. "Come, we have much to discuss." Taking me by the upper arm, he propels me with him.

"All of you need to stop manhandling me." Jerking my arm out of his grasp, I tug at my shirt to straighten it even though it is already perfectly unwrinkled. "I can walk on my own, thank you very much."

"Who is manhandling you?" The word trips Soren's tongue, but the angry power swirling around him scares the shit out of me. "Someone dares touch you without permission?" Obviously, he doesn't count himself in that group. How nice for him.

"No." Zoltan chuckles at my murmured answer. "Let's discuss ... whatever it is that you want, yes?" Smiling sweetly at Soren so I don't punch Zoltan, I practically run past them both.

Seeing the door to the office the rest of them said will be our meeting place, I dash through it like Roberti's hunters are right on my heels. Daren jumps from the chair he is sitting on, both his hands bursting into flickering flames. Tenebris snarls, and Leo hunches over shooting daggers over my shoulder.

"It's just us." Waving my hands like a crazy person, I hurry to calm them down. "Me and the two assholes, I mean." Astara lifts an eyebrow at that last part. "They had a dick measuring contest in the hallway."

"I don't understand what my cock has to do with this,

Francesca." Soren prowls inside the office, the smirk on his face making my hand itch to slap him.

"Okay, you know what? We are not talking about any of your dangly bits." Slashing my hand through the air, I point at a random chair. "Sit your ass down, Soren, and stop this charade."

All the air gets sucked from the room.

I'm either imagining it or everyone else is holding their breath while the ancient Fae looks me up and down as if seeing me for the first time. Humor is dancing in those golden eyes, and without looking away from my gaze, he lowers himself gracefully on the chair I pointed at, expectancy wafting off him in waves.

"What?" When they keep staring at me, I fidget uncomfortably. "That's all I got so far," I tell my feet lamely.

"Don't allow them to tame your spirit, young dragon." My eyes dart to Soren at his softly-spoken words. "They haven't heard how you speak to me until now, no?" Leaning back on the chair, he crosses one ankle over a knee and folds his hands over it. "It would have been much different if I came to see them dressed in that pink glitter skirt you threatened me with. What was it called again?"

"Tutu." Hysterical laughter bursts out of me when all the males in the room look like they just swallowed their tongues. "I'll still do it if you dare to fall asleep before we deal with Roberti and the Board."

"There you are." A proud smile stretches his lips. "I do not like that shrinking daisy you are becoming."

"Violet." When he cocks an eyebrow, I blow out a breath, all the tension leaking out of my body. "The saying is shrinking violet, not daisy." He waves away my comment with a flick of his hand.

"They rest of the Board is hiding something." Soren

gets down to business like he has flipping a switch or something. "I'm considering removing them all, but I cannot do that without finding replacements." He eyes Daren, Leo, and Zoltan with a contemplating look.

"Removing them how?" I blurt out, warnings prickling the back of my skull.

"He plans to kill them," Fenrir says with no inflection in his tone.

"All of them are helping Roberti?" My heart is hammering my ribs for some reason. I want those old farts dead, yes, but now that the possibility is here something holds me back.

"I do not know, and I do not care." Soren waves that damn hand like a queen greeting peasants. "They have failed us all, so they should forfeit their lives."

"You can't just go around killing and replacing people, Soren." Luckily no one comments on the high pitch of my voice.

"Of course I can." The ancient is looking at me like I'm an idiot.

"Like hell you will." Anger makes my hands shake. "Since you are so adamant on killing someone, go kill Roberti. That will fix the majority of our problems." Stepping closer to him, I feel Zoltan move to stand as a sentinel at my back. "Those three jerks will die by my hand only, and only if we have no doubt they are working with him."

"You want them dead." Soren leans forward, his gaze piercing mine. "I feel it in you, child. You can fool them, perhaps, but you can't lie to me."

"I crave their deaths, and all of them know it." Refusing to back down, I stiffen my spine under his observation. "But I will not kill them just because I want it. That will make me no better than them."

I'm not sure when I came to this decision because I sure as hell didn't feel the same when I ran like a child having a tantrum to Soren's rooms. Seeing the boring way the Fae is talking about taking a person's life is like a bucket of icy water over my head, though. No one should be so indifferent about it, no matter how powerful they are. That's what creates monsters like Roberti, who like to play God with all of us.

"And what would you suggest, Francesca?" Soren looks intrigued, like this is all a game to him. Maybe it is.

"We investigate." As soon as the words are out of my mouth, Zoltan snorts.

I elbow him.

"Very well." Soren blinds me with a brilliant smile that makes him look like an eager youngling. "But the moment it gets boring, I shall kill them."

I told the Board once, "No monkeys, no circus." Here comes Francesca the monkey, and if she fails, some innocent people will die. Fuck my life.

Chapter Seventeen

"This is a very stupid idea." Astara mumbles next to me while glancing over her shoulder to make sure Soren can't hear us.

"If you had a better one you, should've said so when you had a chance." Keeping a hand pressed to Tenebris's back, I look around the clearing, avoiding the portal swirling like a gaping hole in front of us.

Everyone on the grounds is hiding. Either the Board had made people stay out of Soren's sight, or they are shitless scared of the ancient Fae, who is right this very moment turning in a circle and staring at everything with wide eyes. How long has he been closed behind walls for a simple stroll outside to make him physically tremble with excitement? I shouldn't feel pity for Soren. Remembering he wants to just kill people that don't tell him what he wants to know is something I have to keep at the front of my mind. Yet, watching him look around in wonder melts my insides. I really am a fool.

"Now what?" Astara breaks through my musings.

"We can go check out the blood banks?" It comes out as a question and she is shaking her head before I'm done talking.

"Soren in the human realm? Have you lost your mind?" I open my mouth, but she slaps a hand over it to silence me. "Zoltan will strangle us both."

I point over her shoulder since I can't speak. Astara turns around, the hold she has on my face loosening. Zoltan is now leaning on the building, his legs crossed at his ankles and his hands tucked in the pockets of his pants. "He will come along." My words are muffled from her hand.

The vampire pushes off the wall, striding to where we are huddled close together like two-year old's whispering out of Soren's ear shot. Childish yes, but necessary. You never know how the Fae will react to anything said out loud. To say that Leo's warning bit me in the ass is the understatement of the century.

"The two of you are up to something." Zoltan says from a few feet away. "I can feel trouble coming from a mile away."

"You were not that far," I throw back, making him smirk.

"I believe they were discussing taking me to the human realm," Soren chirps, the closeness of his voice sending a jolt through my chest. I didn't hear him move.

"You are getting a bell." Soren's eyes cross as he glances at my finger, which is aimed.

He refocuses his gaze on me. "A bell?"

"Francesca does not like it when we sneak up on her without her knowing," Zoltan explains, a permanent smirk etched on his face. "She wishes to turn us all into cats with collars around our necks."

I'm either dreaming, or intrigue is lurking behind

Soren's gaze. The ancient Fae is weird as fuck. Goosebumps cover my arms and he grins at me like the cat that ate the canary, pun intended. Zoltan, on the other hand, yanks on my arm and tucks me behind him, much to Soren's amusement. This whole thing is like a bad dream that I can't wake up from.

"We can check the blood banks, Zoltan." Sidestepping him, I ignore his narrowed stare. "If we come across Roberti with Soren there, it'll be a bonus."

"It's not a bad plan." My jaw hits my chest when he agrees with me. "But we need the others too. It will only serve Roberti's purpose if the humans see Soren walking around them."

"They will not know I'm among them." Soren looks insulted as he squints at Zoltan like he's debating how fast he can kill him.

I step between them and Astara comes shoulder to shoulder with me, both of us acting like a living shield. The males growl low in their chest at the same time. Planting both hands on my hips, I turn from one to the other.

"The two of you knock it off. Right now." Soren pouts, his sudden mood changes enough to give me whiplash. "Zoltan, stop provoking him. It just pisses everyone off." The Fae smiles in victory, but he's a little too soon. "And you can't go around threatening people with or without words. Understood?"

"Or what?" Tilting his head to the side in a way no human being ever would, Soren challenges me, thinking he has the upper hand. Idiot. I spent a few hours earlier coming up with ways to shut him up.

"Or you can enjoy your time awake all on your own." He takes a step back like I just slapped him. "None of us will want to be around you. If you don't like it, go back to sleep, but I have no intention on walking on eggshells because you want to be an ass."

"Well played, young dragon." He nods in approval as if I just passed some weird test of his. "I will behave as you wish."

"Let's go tell the others what we are planning." Zoltan turns, but Soren stops him with a raised hand.

"Not yet," the Fae murmurs, his gaze going strangely unfocused.

Frowning, I lean closer and search his face. Is he a little unhinged? I never gave it much thought, but it can't be good for anyone's sanity to sleep for years or centuries, only having a few moments of wakefulness in between. The slack jaw and empty stare is unnerving to watch. Astara's nails dig into my forearm where she has a punishing grip, and Zoltan is eerily still. Soren snaps out of his daze and flashes an excited smile to all three of us.

"And so it begins," the Fae croons, and he succeeds in confusing the shit out of me.

"Wha—"

All hell breaks loose in this moment, drowning my question. The portal balloons before retracting, the air around us prickling my skin with potent power. It happens so fast I have no time to react. Dozens of hunters spill out from the human realm, scattering around like cockroaches, their white uniforms spreading in the moonlight like a deadly disease. Metal sings through the air and Zoltan tackles me to the ground, both of us rolling away from the dagger that embeds in the spot I just occupied. The hilt shivers violently but stays sunk in the soil, just a sliver from the sharp blade visible above it. The moment we stop, Zoltan taking the brunt of the impact by curling protectively around me, my head swivels around looking for Soren and Astara. I find them in the same position, Astara wide eyed under Soren, who is crouched above her.

"See?" Ignoring the tingles in my belly from having Zoltan's weight on top of me, I jab his side. "Soren has no interest in me, not the way you think. He jumped to protect Astara, not me." Like that's important while hunters are swarming our grounds.

Zoltan grunts something I don't hear.

What I do hear, however, is another blade coming our way. Twisting my hips, I flip us around, avoiding the dagger an inch from Zoltan's head. Straddling his chest, I'm too aware of his hands on my thighs while closing my eyes and concentrating on my breathing. The dragon in me comes to life, stretching my skin painfully. All other sounds are pushed to the background, apart from each move the hunters make. I hear all of them.

I can pinpoint each slide of their feet, each breath they take, as well as the weapons being thrown our way. Familial power prods mine, tentatively at first but much stronger with each passing second. My eyes snap open and I blink fast to get used to all the bright colors swirling around me. My gaze stops on Soren staring at me, sitting similarly above Astara, only he is holding his weight on his knees, unlike me. I have my core pressed to Zoltan's firm abs like an idiot to distract myself. When I try to move, the vampire tightens his hold on my thighs, eliciting a giggle out of me. Leave it to Zoltan to be turned on at a time like this.

My hand shoots out to catch a shuriken in the air. The metal star vibrates between my fingers before I let it loose in the direction it came from. The thump of a body on the ground tells me it hit its mark. Three more thumps follow, and I see Soren's hands blurring in the air as he sends them back as fast as they reach him.

"As much as I love you being on top of me, I think I need to join the fun, Love," Zoltan says, his deep voice sending ripples through his chest that travel right to my core. My channel clenches when I look down at him and see his smoldering gaze.

"Someone warned Roberti that Soren is awake." Rolling away from him, I push to my feet.

"I think that was Soren's plan, Love." Zoltan jumps up too, dusting off his pants. "Whatever happened with the Board, he was baiting them to see if they would betray him."

"He did seem eager to join me and your sister out here." Slinking back under the cover of the trees, I search the open space for any hunters still standing. "This still won't tell him if one or all of the Board members are traitors."

"Depending on what he said to who." He darts his gaze to my face before focusing on our surroundings again. "You'd do well not to underestimate him."

I know that Zoltan is right. But seeing how fast the two of us removed the majority of the hunters makes it difficult to see Soren as anything but an asset. He might be weird and cocky, which has weight behind it judging by the power blasting from him even when he is not trying, but Zoltan knows as much as I do that we need him. Roberti has all our moves mapped out before we even make them. I am no longer the wild card. That honor falls to the ancient Fae, who is having way too much fun at the moment. Poor Astara is clutching Soren's legs like her life depends on it, her eyes running over his naked chest like there is no tomorrow. I've never seen Zoltan's sister so flustered. I'm pretty sure if she wasn't already on her back, she would've fainted when Soren smiled down at her.

"I think your sister is about to hyperventilate." Tilting my chin to point it out, I chuckle at Zoltan's growl.

"Let's go," he hisses, tugging me along with him to circle around and come at the remaining hunter's backs.

My head jerks to the side to see Tenebris has joined us in the forest, his lithe body waving around the trees. He jumped away when the hunters started coming through the portal and blended into the darkness. It must grate on his pride that he isn't the one getting me out of danger since he is, after all, the self-appointed guardian of Francesca Drake. I grin at his snarling face.

"You really are a troublemaker, Love," Zoltan grumbles, shaking his head.

"I don't know what you are talking about." Unable to help myself, my hand caresses his back. I quite enjoy the play of muscles under the thin fabric of his shirt as he moves.

"I'll tell you later." The promise in those words makes me shiver. The dragon in me purrs with anticipation. The dumb bitch doesn't care if she fights or fucks as long as it's fast, hard, and heart pounding. Obviously, Zoltan knows that, too, because he gives me a quick scan that lingers too long on my swaying breasts.

We find the hunters as I expect, plastered behind some extra-wide trunks of trees. They aren't even aware we can see them. Soren, with a slightly dazed Astara following behind him, meet us and we stop for a moment to observe them. Roberti is either stupid or he didn't believe whoever had told him Soren is awake. I can deal with this bunch without any help. They look way too inexperienced to be his elite solders and much too expendable.

"I'm a little insulted," Soren drawls, voicing my thoughts loud enough to spur the hunters into action.

There are a handful still alive, and they try to spread out and corner us from all sides. Tenebris pounces like a lightning bolt, the scream coming out of the closest hunter cut short with the loud crunch of his neck breaking in the panther's jaw. Zoltan is on top of another, wrenching the head off his shoulders, dark red blood gushing out like a spray around him. Soren whirls like a human-shaped tornado, snagging two hunters by their necks and dropping them at his feet bent at unnatural angles. Even their chests are caved in, but I never saw him hit either of them. Astara finally comes out of her hormonal stupor, and her fangs sink deep into a hunter's throat as her eyes glow like lanterns on her pretty face. That leaves one hunter for me, and when he uses his trembling hands to clutch the daggers at his sides, I can't help but smile.

"They sent you here to die." Stepping closer to him, I grin wider when he takes a step back. "What should I do with you? Hmm? Do you want to die fast or slow, hunter? Choose your fate."

"Quit playing with it, Love." Zoltan shakes his hands, which sends blood everywhere. "We have things to do before Andrius guides more of his vermin here."

The hunter's eyes widen at the casual mention of Roberti. I guess the asshole doesn't share how aware we are of what he is doing with his lackeys. Maybe we can use that to our advantage. Soren must've picked up on my hesitation because he comes to stand next to me.

"You wish to let him live," the ancient Fae murmurs for my ears only, but nothing escapes Zoltan.

"It will only make things harder if you send him back." The vampire eyes the hunter with distaste as he twists his full lips.

"Go before I change my mind," I snap at the hunter,

and he doesn't wait to be told twice. "Tell Roberti I'm coming for him," I call at his retreating back.

"You know he might hide, Love." Zoltan chuckles at the sprinting hunter diving head-first through the portal.

"But he *is* arrogant enough to be pissed and come face me himself." At least I hope that will be the case.

"Cunning." My lips twitch at the admiration in Zoltan's voice.

"Just tired of bullshit, Daywalker. Nothing more, nothing less." The swirling colors disappear as my dragon retreats inside me.

"I do not envy you, Zoltan." Soren snickers, throwing an arm over Astara's shoulders.

My friend turns to me grinning like a fool so the Fae doesn't see her. I can't stop the giggle from coming out of my lips.

"We shall face the demigod in the human realm?" Soren looks at Zoltan over Astara's head.

"Yes, we will." I'm the one who answers him as I stride toward the building. "And this time, I'm planning on ripping his throat out with my teeth." Tenebris's cry punctuates the venom in my words.

"Woot!" Astara shrieks, running from under the Fae's arm to join me, Zoltan's laughter echoing around the trees.

"It's a good time to be awake." Soren chortles, his steps much lighter now than when we were moving to the portal.

It's a miracle what a little killing can do to improve a Fae's mood.

Chapter Eighteen

"It's like we are at a funeral," I tell the room since no one has said a word in the last hour.

Okay, maybe it has only been ten minutes since we piled into the warded dining room, but it sure as all hells feels like days have passed. No, we are sprawled around the space, all sitting and eyeing each other like we are in a stand-off in one of those old western movies humans love so much. Yes, I've seen some of those, too. Back when the Daywalkers didn't know I existed, my life outside of work included dates with my television and the bottle. I was popular like that.

"I'm sorry I'm late." Argoz hastens through the doors, unceremoniously dropping into an empty chair. Zoltan had sent him somewhere after whispering something in his ear with urgency, so apparently, we had been waiting on the ghoul to return to continue with this meeting. "All three of them are still locked up in the meeting chamber." Argoz tugs on the collar of his shirt. "There were shouts but they have a confusion spell around it, so I couldn't understand a word that was said."

"Useless," Soren huffs, looking at the ghoul as if his presence here will soil us somehow.

"Don't be rude," I snap at him, and the Fae pouts.

It's adorable for a second, but then his eyes dart to Zoltan and the vampire snarls. Like a two-year-old, the ancient Fae is baiting Zoltan just to get a reaction out of him. It's annoying as fuck. At least Soren drops the act when I give him a narrowed-eye stare down. With a twinkle in his orange irises, he leans back and stretches both arms behind them, resting them on the back of the sofa he claimed for himself.

"There will be more hunters coming soon." Reminding them why we are gathered here, I look from face to face. "What's our plan?"

I don't tell them I'm itching to get going and find that miserable fuck Roberti. Zoltan bringing me back here might've calmed my fury a little, but it's still simmering inside me like a ticking bomb about to go off any moment. The longer I linger here, the bigger the chance I'll explode around unsuspecting bystanders. The last thing I need is to hurt people who don't deserve it. Even if they are working with Roberti, I still blame him for manipulating them. He did the same to me, after all, so it's definitely all his fault.

"If you did what you were supposed to, things would be different now," Soren says directly to Fenrir, and my friend clenches his jaw.

I squint at Soren.

"What was that?" At my question, the powerful Fae waves me off like I'm a pesky fly. "Soren?" Pushing his name through grinding teeth, I curl my fingers so I don't jump on him and strangle him where he sits.

"He was meant to seduce you and bond with you," Daren answers me and my eyebrows crawl all the way up to my hairline. "I didn't know, but you'd have to be stupid not to figure it out." The mage lifts both hands, his palms up pointed toward the sky in surrender.

"She is a Dragon Blood. She needs to be bonded to a Fae." Soren sniffs like the pompous ass he is, his chin jutting out.

"Oh, hells to the no." Jolting out of my chair, I stab a finger at his face. "You screwed me over by blood bonding with me and tying my life to yours. Like fuck I'll let you have a say about who I do or do not bond with otherwise."

"It is not too late to fix it." Soren eagerly leans forward, somehow oblivious that I'm about to scratch his eyes out. "If a proper Fae bond is created, the one with Zoltan will dissolve. It's still new from what I can sense. You will not feel pain, I assure you."

"No, but you will. I promise you." Goosebumps pop up on my arms when I hear my own voice.

Or maybe it's from the suffocating silence Zoltan is emanating right now. Heat blasts me from behind from the vampire, burning my back so much that standing in the middle of an inferno will probably be less painful. Deep down, something inside me is screaming at me to calm the situation or someone will die. Knowing how insanely powerful Soren is, I'm not willing to test Zoltan's strength against him.

"I thought you were different than the rest of the Board, Soren." Taking deep breaths to stop the raging storm brewing in my chest, I roll my shoulders.

"How so?" One perfect eyebrow cocks, but I can tell he is not being an ass. He truly is curious.

"You can't force people to do things just because you think it's best." Scrubbing a hand over my face, I sigh deeply, letting all the fight drain from me. I'm so freaking tired I want to sleep for a decade. "You've sacrificed more than anyone ever should by keeping this place alive with your own life force. I'm sorry you had to do that, but Soren … Fenrir, me … we are not objects for you to move around a game board. Fenrir's heart was taken long before he met me. Would you wish to break it by denying him love?"

The shock on Fenrir's face would be comical if the situation was not so fucked up. I'm still upset with him for being a bully and an asshole toward Myst, but only a moron wouldn't see the feelings both of them are trying to hide from each other. I wonder if Zoltan and I do the same—or did the same I should say.

"What a foolish sentiment. Love is for humans, young dragon." Soren's eyes glow like fires on his face. "We are predators and we choose the strongest mate. One that can make us more powerful."

A low growl comes from deep within Zoltan's chest.

Everyone is frozen like they are praying their presence goes unnoticed in the room. I can't blame them. Soren stupidly poked the bear instead of discussing the hunters and Roberti. I kind of expected time to not have the same meaning to the powerful Fae as it does to us, but I never thought it would bring more problems than solutions.

"You sound just like Andrius." Soren jerks back like I've slapped him. "It's all about power. Being on top of the food chain. To hells with people's lives and who we destroy in the process, huh?" Shaking my head, I fold my arms over my chest more to keep my ribcage from fracturing open than anything else. "I don't want any part of that, Soren. I'll walk right into the first hunter's blade before I turn into someone like that."

A jolt goes through me when, for a split second, I think Soren's lips twitch at the corners. I blink stupidly at him, but it's gone so fast I probably imagined it. His head tilts in that strange way as he considers me. I'm too scared to turn around and check on Zoltan because I don't know what I will see, but I'm pretty sure the vampire is not even breathing right now.

"The rest of the Board will disagree." Soren's shoulders relax and he rests his back on the sofa. "You are too powerful for them to let you choose your mate."

"No one is asking them." I have no idea why we are having this conversation. It has nothing to do with Roberti, or the old farts for that matter. The Fae is just trying his best to be an incredibly big pain in my ass, to be honest.

"Ah, but that's where you are wrong." Crossing one ankle over the opposite knee, Soren smiles at Zoltan over my shoulder. It's the most terrifying smile I've ever seen. "If I am not mistaken, they are looking into separating your bond as we speak. They can control both of you better like that."

My mouth opens to tell him off, or whatever else comes to mind, but vertigo hits me so suddenly I'm instantly numb from it. Chill spreads through my limbs until they feel like blocks of ice, and I sink down, my knees bending as I go. Shouts ring through the room, but they are muffled and sound like they are coming from under a vast body of water. Movements blur around me, the room spinning so much the rest of my body is pulled down as the ground comes to meet me.

Zoltan stops my fall. I can't feel his skin in this frozen prison that is my body, but I recognize him on a whole new level. An unexplainable knowing courses through me. He will always catch me if I fall. The thought is enlightening, and in that moment, I realize I hadn't been fighting my feelings for the Daywalker. I'd been deceiving myself, making myself believe I didn't trust me. I do, though, and I always will.

My gaze locks on Soren.

Dread slithers up my spine until the back of my neck tingles from it. An intent look crosses the ancient Fae's face. He doesn't look worried, or even excited that I'm about to die if the ice spreading through me reaches my heart. With each panful breath that shreds my lungs, I know I have only moments before I part with this world. The blood barely moves through my veins, and it's curdling so much that each beat of my heart feels like it will tear them apart. No, he is neither worried nor excited.

Soren is expectant.

Excruciating pain pierces the cotton clogging my ears. A strangled cry is wrenched from my lips, the center of my chest burning. The agony brings sound. Everyone yells at each other, all of them loudly voicing what needs to be done. I desperately sink into myself and search for that cord that connects me to Zoltan. Fear makes me grab it and yank it as deep within my soul as I can. He grunts but says nothing else, only tightens his arms around me as if he can physically stop what is happening.

How didn't I see this coming?

My mental grasp on the bond is slipping. Tenebris keeps popping in and out of sight as he paces in agitation, his occasional screech grating on my nerves. Red and green magic swirls around my body as Daren sends pulse after pulse of what I assume is a shield to protect me. I can't muster the strength to tell him it isn't working.

"Why are we standing here." Leo's snarl is filled with so much hatred he sounds more like a beast than a male. "I will rip them to shreds with my bare hands."

"Hellion, can you hear me?" Fenrir's face appears above

me, his eyes black with a white pupil. "Just blink if you understand what I'm saying." My eyeballs are on fire when I do what he says. "Let your dragon fight the foreign magic."

My gaze flicks to Soren and I see him leaning forward, too, watching us like this is a show created for his entertainment. What possessed me to think this creature will actually help us is beyond me, but it's too late to go back now. I always knew my impulsiveness would be the death of me, though I'd hoped I'd go out with a bang mid-battle or something equally as valiant. Not like this. Not while I lay on the floor in a pitiful heap.

"How ..." I croak, wincing at the pain stabbing my throat. "How do you know-it's magic?"

"I can sense my father's essence," Daren spits angrily, not opening his eyes. Lines of concertation are etched on his skin, the corners of his mouth pulling down. "It's not just his own." Sweat is beading on his hairline and upper lip.

Zoltan still says nothing.

"She can try and fight it," Soren says conversationally, an amused tone in his voice. "Or you can kill the Board and stop them from severing the bond entirely." He waves a hand nonchalantly as if discussing the weather. "Zoltan can repair it if he so wishes."

"You know we can't kill any of them unless someone is ready to take their place." Fenrir glares at the other Fae, much to Soren's delight. "The disbalance of power will kill us all and bring Sienna down with it."

Fuck me running. This is the first time I hear this, and if not for the excruciating pain barreling through me, I might be pissed that nobody thought it was important to tell me that little nugget of wisdom. Sucking in air so I can tell them all to go fuck themselves for continuing to lie to me and omit things, another scream is ripped from my throat when something claws at my spirit. It's vile and foreign, invading my being like some disease.

"I'll take Silas's place," Astara says calmly, and my head jerks in her direction as all my pain is forgotten.

No, no, no, I scream in my head, but no words come out.

"I'll step up for the shifters." Leo growls, his wolf speaking through the alpha's lips.

Goosebumps cover me from head to toe. *Please, no!* The screams are in my mind only, not a single sound coming out to stop them. I'm the one who should be sacrificing myself for this insanity. Not the people I've done everything I can to protect. *I am the half blood, it's me that doesn't matter,* I want to tell them, to shout it in their face, but I stare mutely while my soul is melted by an invisible foe. I'm just grateful that—

"I will take my father's place." Daren's voice cuts through my thoughts and nothing stops the wailing scream coming from my chest.

I'm silenced by Zoltan's hot lips pressing on mine. My skin is so cold that it hurts where we touch, but that doesn't stop me from opening my mouth and letting his tongue in. *At least I'll die with his taste on my lips,* I think stupidly, delirious from the torture I'm enduring. It doesn't last long, and when he pulls away he takes my breath with him.

"I will be the one that kills them." Bright burning irises in the shape of the sun seer into mine. I realize the terrifying voice that sounds like the parts of a mountain rolling down and grinding stone on stone comes from Zoltan.

Chapter Nineteen

They left me. Locked in my own body, I can't believe what happened.

The moment all of them, including Tenebris, left the dining hall in a rush, all the pain disappeared. Oh, those vile claws are still clutching my soul and tugging on the bond I have with Zoltan like their life depends on it, but everything else is gone. My body is still a block of ice burning with an inferno on the inside, but it no longer hurts. A shadow flickering in my peripheral vision gets my attention, and my heart lodges in my throat when I realize not all of them are gone.

With his head cocked to the side and his silver hair falling like a waterfall over his bare wide shoulders, Soren is observing me like I'm a bug under a microscope. Anger surges through me because he just sits there like all this is a joke. Having him awake and talking is something I regret with each passing moment.

"You are angry with me, child," Soren says softly, a line

between his eyebrows disturbing the perfection that is his face.

I can't speak because my lips are glued together, luckily. Otherwise, he'd hear all the profanities I'm spitting at him in my head. But I'm pretty sure my glare is burning a hole in the middle of his forehead right now. By the widening of his eyes, he knows it too.

"You were never in danger." Looking insulted, confusion and something else I can't name are fighting for dominance over his features. "This was the least painful way of setting things right."

Since I still can't speak, I glare harder. It's a promise of what I'll do to him the moment I can move my limbs again. Daren told me I've been fighting to gain control over my life since the day I was born. Maybe I have. But nothing, absolutely nothing compares to this moment when I'm just a passenger in my unmovable body, unable to do anything besides breathe. A crazy thought hits me out of nowhere. This is how humans feel when facing one of us. Crippled between their fear and our powers, no one hears their internal screams. The Accord was signed for a reason, a reason Roberti is shitting on right now.

"You have to see that what I did was for the best." Standing from the sofa in a fluid move, Soren folds his hands at the small of his back, his bare feet padding silently around me. "They needed motivation, Zoltan more than the rest of them. I found the best solution to the problem we are facing."

Apprehension wriggles like a coiled snake in my stomach. What he did? What the fuck? What exactly did he do apart from goading Zoltan's anger by flirting with me and then talking shit about our bond? I'm missing something here. Fury burns inside me because I can't do jack shit about it but blink at the Fae.

"You see, they were corrupt."

Soren is talking to himself, completely oblivious to the internal battle I'm having while sprawled at his feet. *I'm going to shave your head and leave you bald, you asshole.* Using my eyes, I try to burn that thought through his eyes. Even with all my efforts, I get zero reaction.

"Not all of them were in cahoots with the child demigod, but"—One graceful finger flicks in the air in front of him— "none attempted to stop him, either. I believed having you here would bring the culprit to light, but I was mistaken."

I wish I could laugh at how incredulous he looks at the idea of him making a mistake. All that sleep has screwed Soren's brain six ways to Sunday. The Fae is as nuts as a squirrel, and I made sure he was aware enough of all the goings on to turn psycho on all of us. Like Roberti was not enough of a problem, I added a new flavor to the shitshow stirring in the pot. *Good job Franky, you dumbass.*

I might be as crazy as him.

"You, young dragon, almost made all my efforts futile when you thought pushing Zoltan away was to protect him." All my thoughts screech to a halt at that. "Your bond should've been much stronger by now." Scowling at me like a teacher that has caught me cheating, he wiggles a finger and shakes his head. "If I tug a little harder, it'll break apart."

Say what now?

My eyes are about to pop out of their sockets when realization hits me like a sledgehammer to the back of my head. The pain, the magic, the vile claws scratching my soul and clawing at the bond is not from the Board members trying to break it. It's from Soren playing games with me once again. As if tying my life to this stupid place was not enough. My dragon, which has been nowhere to be found until now, finally wakes, poking its surreptitious head out. The magic is trying to pulse like it always does but whatever has me frozen in a statue-like state prevents it. I can feel the bitch's annoyance, and she joins me in my loathing of the Fae, who is still circling us.

The floor under me lurches violently, flinging me around like a rag doll. My face is introduced to the hard floor, my cheekbone smarting when it smacks hard with the sound of a watermelon dripping. Soren stops pacing, unfazed by the tremors rocking the foundations of the building. The tall, arched windows release ominous crackling sounds, the glass not shattering but spreading slowly to form cracks that look like cobwebs. Holding my breath, my gaze darts around because I think I caused it to happen. Screams, roars, and hundreds of stomping boots tell me otherwise.

A serene smile spreads over Soren's face.

"It has started." He squares his shoulders, his head swiveling around as if he expects applause for his statement.

In the meantime, I'm screaming inside my head *What started? What the fuck did you do you crazy asshat!* That's when my entire existence comes to a halt. A rage-filled roar that's so loud it makes my ears bleed silences everything in the academy. My survival instinct snaps into action, the dragon inside me sending a blast of magic out to destroy whatever hold Soren has over me. The windows rattle harshly before exploding outward, millions of tiny pieces of glass showering the gravel around in a tinkling downpour.

One second, I'm on the floor.

The next, I'm facing Soren.

Knees slightly bent, shoulders hunched and ready to pounce on the crazy ass, I lock my gaze on his. Colors burst to life, dancing and twining around us, every life force revealing itself to me. My irises contract and expand, Soren's features coming into a sharp focus. His airbrushed skin shows the pores that, until now, were invisible to me. Through the curtain of hair falling over my face, I track every breath he takes, every slight shift of weight on his feet.

The severity of his orange orbs, which are focused on me, should make me want to run and hide, but I'm way past that point. The roar that broke every window in this building belongs to Zoltan. And I'm going to level this damn town myself if any harm has come to him. All because of the Fae standing a few feet away from me. The monstrosity living inside me and I are finally in an agreement.

Death will feast tonight in these halls.

"An sin tha thu, dràgon òg," Soren purrs, raising the hairs on my arms at attention.

Strangely enough, his words translate through my mind. "There you are, young dragon." If I didn't know better, I'd think this charade, all the hurt that will follow after tonight is over, every bit of it has been done to get a reaction from my Dragon Blood. To what end will Soren destroy the lives of those I care about? The answer isn't important. It's obvious we have very different opinions on what is accept-able in this situation.

"Dé an seann duine a tha agad." My head tilts the same way Soren's did earlier when he was observing me, thick strands of hair falling over my face.

"You are calling me old?" The Fae's chuckle is humor-less. It rakes through my nerves like nails on a chalkboard.

We circle each other.

"Why?" My dragon is itching for a fight. I'll let her have it.

But I, Francesca the stupid half-blood who lets everyone walk all over her, need to know this. Why would the one person I ran to for help turn on me and stab me in the back? For some idiotic reason, this is a worse betrayal than the one coming from Roberti. At least I never allowed that jerk to see me cry.

Soren grins, curdling the blood in my veins.

Power slams into me like a tsunami, flinging me through the air and sending my body through the thick wall separating the dining hall and whatever room is next to it. The broken edges of bricks and pieces of plaster tear through my skin, sending waves of agony piercing my chest. A shrill scream—more from anger than hurt—rips my vocal cords apart, but from somewhere deep in the academy, Zoltan answers me, Tenebris's terrifying cry following.

At least they are still alive.

Crawling on my knees, I sit on my haunches and yank the thumb from my right hand back in place. It got twisted in the fall and was touching the back of my hand. My teeth grind when the bone cracks, heat surging through it as the break heals. Staggering to my feet, I roll my neck. Soren waits in the same spot, parts of the wall I went through falling between us and hitting the floor in a cloud of dust billowing through the air.

Sadness spreads through me at the thought that it'll all end like this. Call me a romantic fool, but I always thought if I died, I'd go fighting at Zoltan's side and taking an enemy down with me. No matter how hard I try, even after all this insanity, I truly don't hate Soren. In his messed-up mind, I'm sure everything makes sense to him, even if it is crazy for the rest of us.

The building lurches again and even more broken pieces of the wall tumble to the floor. With a slight bounce on the balls of my feet, I pounce through the opening right at Soren, moving faster than a supernatural should be able to do. It's almost like gravity has a different hold on my body and the laws of physics don't apply the same to dragon bloods. My body collides with his, taking him by surprise if the boggled expression is any indication. Latching onto his neck with both hands, I wrap my legs around his torso and squeeze for all I'm worth.

Bones give way under my assault, the popping sounds like bullets passing through a silencer reaching my ears. A startled shout comes from Soren as we both go down, rolling around the dust-covered ground. His hands grip my thighs, his fingers digging into the muscles there in hopes to force me to release him.

I tighten my legs harder.

Our tumble ends with Soren above me, his weight pressing me hard to the unforgiving floor. My spine protests, but I cling to him like a monkey, my nails tearing the skin of his throat the harder I squeeze. No one, not even him, will have the last say in this clusterfuck that is my life. Since me and the crazy Fae are tied together, I guess I'll be killing us both. Maybe Roberti will rethink his actions if there is no Dragon Blood feeding magic to this damn place.

Soren's face twists in a grimace.

A pulse of magic flings from me into him, making us both gasp and groan in pain. The anger is turning my vision blurry, everything around me bathed in the red of my rage. *Kill, kill, kill* … The word plays on repeat, and it makes my ears thunder from inside my skull. Soren is trembling in my hold.

No, wait.

He is quaking above me, but the Fae is definitely not trembling. The fucking asshole is laughing, his whole body shaking with it. My grip on him slackens from the absurdity of it, my jaw unhinging when the snicker bellows as a laugh-out-loud chortle. I gape while he looks down at me, his long silver hair falling on both sides of my face like a curtain, leaving us hidden from the outside world and face to face. His orange irises glow with happiness while I stupidly gawk at him. Blood is trickling from the corners of his full, bow-shaped lips and from his perfect nose. There is even a visible fracture from his hairline down to his temple on the right side of his face.

And he is guffawing like a freak in my face.

"Now you are ready, Francesca," he chirps between bursts of laughter, pushing strands of hair out of my eyes. "Just like Zoltan, you needed a little motivation as well."

"You are deranged," I deadpan, still unable to pick my jaw up and close my mouth.

"Bah." Soren is conversational, while my mind is reeling from the twist in events. Why isn't he dying or fighting me? "Sanity is overrated." His weight shifts and he settles more firmly between my legs as a new apprehension stabs me through the chest. My eyes narrow on his stupid face. "What you needed is to lose the tight control you were clinging to. Now you can face a Titan without me worrying about either of our lives."

"What are you talking about?" Unclenching my stiff fingers from around his neck, I wiggle and kick to get him off me. "You were supposed to help us deal with everything. Instead, you fucked up all of our lives."

"Disease has spread through the veins of the academy, young dragon." Rolling off me, Soren props himself on one elbow and flicks his silky, silver hair over his shoulder. "The heart of Sienna cried for a cure. I simply gave it the best medicine I have." At my confused look, he snickers. "I gave it a new Board. One that is not greedy for power or too afraid to lose it with a new change."

"You are part of the Board. You know that right?" Talking slowly to get through his thick skull, I cock an eyebrow. "I have no intention of playing sleeping beauty for the next millennia." At his surprised jerk, I slash a hand through the air. "No fucking way I'm taking your place. I'll kill myself first."

"I do not wish to perish." Scrunching up his forehead, he eyes me contemplatively.

"You'll perish right now if you don't start talking because I'll rip your heart out." Snarling, I clench my fists. "You destroyed everything, you stupid old fuck."

"I did not." His chin juts out. "I will prove it."

Jumping to his feet, which should've been impossible because of his caved-in ribs and all the blood flowing from him, Soren saunters across the destroyed dining hall, aiming straight for the doors. I stand frozen while I stare at his back.

"Come along now." Throwing the words over his shoulder, he doesn't slow to wait for me.

It takes me exactly two seconds before I'm dashing right behind him, though I admit I'm dreading whatever it is he wants me to find out.

Chapter Twenty

I'm practically jogging after Soren, growing more stupefied with each step as I watch his body heal without causing as much as a pause in his glide. Because he is not walking, he is gliding through the hallways, his bare feet expertly missing all the sharp, broken pieces littering the ground. On the other hand, I sound like a stampede of elephants as I try to keep up with the crazy jerk.

"Something is holding them up," Soren mutters to his nose, slipping further away from me.

Adding a burst of speed so he doesn't leave my sight, my wild gaze takes in all the destruction, as well as the people running around. Dizziness comes out of nowhere and my hand shoots out and I catch myself on a wall before I have the chance to fall to the soiled floor like a chopped off stump. Subconsciously, my fist rubs between my breasts, a coil tightening at the center of my chest. It takes a moment to realize why I feel like emptying my stomach.

"Get your fucking claws out of my bond." My snarl stops Soren in his tracks.

Spinning on his heel, he considers me from afar before giving me a slow once over, his eyes traveling over my body from head to toe. "Your bond?" One graceful finger scratches his chiseled jaw. "You are welcome for that, by the way." With a nod, he turns his back and disappears around the corner.

Screw dizziness.

Bolting down the hall, I take a sharp turn and collide with his bare back, almost falling on my ass. When I realize I'm clutching the waistband of his silky pants and pulling them low enough to see the tops of the globes that form his perky backside, I jerk my hands away as if I've been burned.

"What do you mean I'm welcome?" Hissing at the Fae, I tiptoe so I can see over his shoulder.

My heart skips a beat.

The stupid organ jackhammers next, jumping first to the roof of my mouth before plunging to my feet. My lungs shrivel when all the oxygen in the building gets sucked out. Who cares about Soren's ass? Not me, apparently, because my fingers twist in the waistband of his silky pants as I yank him firmly in front of me like a living shield.

"What the fuck is that?" Breathing the words, I'm praying whatever it is it doesn't hear me.

Soren, the jerk, snorts.

I backhand the base of his skull before taking a firmer grip on his pants. His growl tells me he doesn't appreciate my hands-on explanation of how happy I am that he is amused. See how much I give a shit.

Someone ... well let me rephrase that, *something* is standing in the middle of the wide-open foyer at the entrance of the academy. At eight and a half feet tall, it's humanoid in form, but that's where the similarities end. Skin as black as obsidian shines in the moonlight streaming through the shattered windows. Thighs twice as wide as my shoulders are spread shoulder-width apart, the thing's ass flexing as it shifts from foot to foot. Muscles have muscles on the creature's back, all outlines with shadows cast from the floating flames flickering around it on the walls. Tree trunk arms bulge when it rolls its neck and they end in hands as wide as my chest tipped with vicious, dagger-sharp claws.

The creature moves its head to the side, ebony straight hair caressing its back all the way to its buttocks. A glinting horn juts out of its temple, curling around its head like a crown made of bone. It's slightly lighter in color from the hair deceiving the eye and hiding the horn from view, so I didn't notice it at first. I see it now.

Oh, dear fates, how clearly I see it. And poor Tenebris is within reach, snarling like a feral cat poised to strike. *'Please don't die, Tenebris. Please.'* I beg the shifter with everything in me.

"I see." Soren snorts.

"What is it?" Jerking on his pants, I hear the silky fabric ripping under my fingers. "What do you see? Speak, Soren, before that thing turns around and kills us." An invisible spear stabs me between my shoulder blades. "Is it a Titian? Did Roberti send a Titian here?"

We are fucked.

Soren, the deranged Fae, throws his head back and chortles so loud the creature stiffens.

"What the fuck is the matter with you." Slapping a hand over his mouth, I don't dare breathe.

Swearing is kind of my thing. Why pussyfoot around using words I don't mean when everyone knows I say fuck at least once an hour? But my usage of the preferred senti- ment has exceeded my normal quota tonight. Because seri- ously, what the fuck?

"It's not a Titan." Soren's words are muffled through my hand.

"What is it?" Murmuring through numb lips, I wonder why the bitch living inside me doesn't even stir. She is usually the first to perk up when danger is staring us in the face.

And it will be staring in three, two … yup.

The creature turns to face us and my knees buckle as gravity returns full force and pulls me down. Soren reacts fast, snatching me around my waist to hold me up, his pants twisting because I still haven't let them go.

"Zoltan." I'm not sure I say it out loud, but I know my lips are moving.

"Meet your mate, young dragon," Soren whispers in my ear, his words penetrating the white noise there.

I want to run.

But I can't move because my body is locked in place from the terror coursing through me. A predator has me in its sights and it will pounce the second I twitch a muscle. But I want to. Really bad.

Tenebris slinks closer and my gaze flashes to him. He wasn't snarling at Zoltan. He is baring his teeth at something in front of him. I can't focus on what it is now, though, because my eyes are searching the obsidian creature with Zoltan's face. It's horrifyingly beautiful with its shimmering black skin stretched over cheekbones sharp enough to cut glass. His lips part and the tips of his fangs poke from under his top one, those blue orbs I recognize immediately searching my face.

His hands keep clenching and he shuffles his feet as if not knowing if he should come closer or walk away. Soren's voice breaks through my fear and panic, finally unlocking my stiff muscles.

"He was the first," the ancient Fae tells me. "Older than Silas or any vampire alive."

I scan the horns circling Zoltan's head, a crown from twisted bone that suits him more than I'd like to admit right now. Until my eyes drop below his waist and I stare at his jutting appendance, which is as long as my arm and is pointing right at me. My gaze jerks back to his face and I forget how scared I am.

"If that thing comes anywhere near me, I'll chop it off." Stabbing a shaking finger at said thing, I swallow thickly.

Zoltan barks out a startled laugh, the sound further easing the horror-movie scenarios that have been playing in my head. And then guilt slams me like a bucket of cold water when I see the wariness in his eyes mixing with … acceptance, maybe? Or is it resignation? Tendons jump under the skin of his forearms as he lifts his arm toward me before dropping it to his side. *Who are you to judge, half-blood?* The sneer in my head is a slap to the face. The vampire's body turns slightly, moving to face whoever it was he was squaring off with before we arrived.

"Zoltan." My shout snaps his head in my direction. Pushing down prejudice or whatever the hell made me react to him the way I did, I untangle myself from Soren, jutting my chin in a dare for him to fight me on what I'm about to say. "I want the bond." His eyes widen. "I swear it."

His chest expands and the sigh coming out of him breaks my heart. I said those words while I was naked and writhing on his bed under him, but I think he finally knows I meant it then as I mean it now. We might not even live long enough to regret anything, least of all bonds. Screw Soren and his comments about love being a human thing. My lips part to say more.

Zoltan hunches, his body shuddering as he sidesteps

whatever causes the reaction, which reveals what his large body has been hiding. Two domes of magic pressing against each other, one burning a sickly green color and the other a familiar lava red I've seen coming from Daren's hands are pulsing and battling each other, sending stray sparks all over the place. And Soren is still yapping next to me.

"You see, he sacrificed his right to bond a mate because he loathed his other form." The Fae sniffs as if not wanting to be a monster is stupid and below him. I spear him with a side-eyed glance. "He chose to remain as you knew him, which allowed Silas to lord over power like that. But he only needed motivation, as I said."

"Making him jealous is hardly a motivation for accepting something he turned his back on centuries ago." All my attention is on Daren and his father, who are having some kind of magical stand-off.

"Millennia. Several, as a matter a fact." Soren waves me off when I gape at him. "And jealousy is hardly what pushed him over the edge."

"What pushed him?" Mind reeling, I'm not sure if I should join the fight or hear more of what Soren is saying.

"A woman." One side of his lips tilts up as he is giving me a pointed look, satisfaction plastered all over his face. "A woman always does, young dragon."

"Great," I grumble, inching away from him. "Add more shit to the list of sins I have committed against those I care about."

"Things are being set to rights." Folding his arms across his chest, he glares down his nose at me down.

"At what cost, you dumb jerk?" Deciding I would rather fight the Board than bicker with Soren, I stomp away, the Fae shadowing me. "How many more people need to die so things are set to right in your world, huh?" I don't turn around because I can feel his breath on the top of my head. This one has no concept of personal space.

"As many as it takes so that there is balance between the worlds." Soren sounds like a mad scientist who has been using the rest of us as his test subjects. "We will have the victory. I made sure of it."

"No victory is worth the blood of the ones you care about, Soren." Astara and Leo move behind Daren looking for an opening to jump on Silas and the shifter, who are cowering behind Daren's father. "When you understand that, I will actually take your word for what it is. Until then … I regret that I woke you up."

"You don't mean that." When the hurt is obvious in his softly-spoken words, I peer at him over my shoulder. "You are blood of my blood. You don't mean what you are saying."

"I do, Soren." Tears prickle the corners of my eyes at the stricken look on his perfect face. "I'm sorry I woke you up."

Chapter Twenty-One

Movement catches my attention and my head snaps back to the mages. The shifter Board member has shifted, his wolf as large as a horse and his gray fur sprinkled with white. One of the eyes on the animal is milky white, and it gives the shifter a sinister appearance, one that is not visible when he is in human form. He lifts on his hind legs, bringing his head above Daren's father's so he can snarl at Leo. My carefree friend who is always up for sharing a joke or lightening things up is nowhere to be found. In his place is an alpha wolf facing the old shifter, his upper lip curled over canines as long as my forearm.

Why is everyone doubling in size? I wonder as I quicken my steps. Daren's outstretched arms tremble in front of him. Yup. They definitely need help. Someone bumps into my legs and I look down at Tenebris, who is slinking beside me while partially covering me with his shoulders. My hand sinks into his fur, the physical contact I used to hate now grounding me. A large hand blocks my path, and Zoltan comes closer to us, as well.

"We can go around it." When Zoltan looks down at me, I point at the wide stairway leading to the upper floors. "If you create a distraction, Tenebris and I can jump them from above."

He is already shaking his head, his long hair sliding over his shoulders, making my fingers twitch to touch it and see if it's as silky as it looks. The vampire has a lot of explaining to do ... later. Grinding my teeth, I ignore Soren lurking and listening intently to each word spoken. As if he wasn't weird enough before this.

"Fine, I'll create a distraction, you go jump them." How Zoltan can look arrogant even while resembling a monster is beyond me. "Exactly, you can't because you are huge. Now go do something so they don't see us."

Not waiting for an answer, and not getting one, I nudge Tenebris and we peel away from Soren and the vampire. With a glare that would've made me pee my pants ten minutes ago, Zoltan whirls around and roars at the Board members, taking his frustration out on them.

"We should keep one of the old farts alive so he can scream at them when I piss him off." Huffing as I run up the stairs, I grin when the panther snorts out a laugh. "This way." Veering to the left at the second floor landing, I dash around the ornate railing, peeking down to find the perfect spot.

"Something doesn't feel right." I jump out of my skin when Soren mutters behind me.

"What? Things are not going the way you lined them up?" Hissing at him under my breath, I lean over to judge the distance for my jump to put me on top of Silas. I want that sucker squished under my feet.

"Don't you feel the energy, young dragon." Ignoring my animosity, he frowns as he stares below us.

"Stop calling me young dragon, and what kind of energy?" Better safe than sorry. I hold Tenebris back with a fistful of fur and close my eyes to search for whatever has Soren so disturbed.

I feel the slimy power in an instant and recoil from it.

Pressing harder on the wooden banister, I search for anyone or anything that could be inside the academy and causing this. The gray wolf spins in a circle as if he can sense us watching him from above. The swipe of Zoltan's sharp claws makes the old fart turn his way, and that's when I catch a glimpse of the necklace swinging around his neck, which up until this point was hidden by his shaggy fur." My blood turns to ice when I zero in on the emblem.

A lightening bolt separating two axes set in a triangle, which is the same one burned into my retinas from the hood of the car the hunters used to blow us up. Soren is definitely observant, the Fae following my line of sight faster than I can blink. The unnatural way he stills unnerves me to no end, but it also tells me he knows something I'm dying to find out.

"What does it mean?" I don't need to explain what I'm asking about.

"It's a symbol of two Titans." The wood cracks under my grip at the murmured words coming from Soren. "Perses, the Titan of destruction, and Menoetius, the Titan of violent anger and mortality."

"I have a feeling you are not telling me everything." When those orange eyes flick to mine, I bare my teeth. "You never do."

"I was the one that forced those two into their prison." Holding my gaze for the first time, Soren looks troubled. "Somehow, I missed that this was personal."

"Welcome to my life." I fake clinking a glass in cheers,

my fist bumping the air between us. "Stick around, we will make sure you regret being alive. It's a perk of mine."

The Fae is watching me like I've grown a second head, but shouts from below tell me I'm out of time for chitchats. Releasing Tenebris, who has been tugging stubbornly to be freed from the hold I have on him, I take a few steps back, Soren follows me, his eyebrows dipping low over his eyes. I grin at the ancient Fae before sprinting at the banister, the panther bolting along with me. We float suspended in the air for a heart-stopping moment before plummeting down.

Landing on top of Silas and taking the jerk down might be the most satisfying thing I've done in my life. The old vampire sneers at me from the ground, but the heel of my boot wipes that off in a second. His nose shatters, dark blood gushing over his mouth and chin and soaking up his robes. I flinch when instead of Leo, Soren wraps his legs around the gray wolf and flips, him on the floor. The old fart doesn't stand a chance when Soren sinks his fingers into the wolf's throat and gracefully lifts him in the air. Instead of killing him, the Fae hands him to the alpha, and I swallow bile when Leo tears into the Board member's throat with gusto. Soren rips his palm open, slapping his hand over the weeping wound on Leo's shoulder. My friend stiffens and his eyes bulge.

Hands wrap around my knees and pull me down. All the air rushes out of my lungs when my back hits the floor. Curling my knees to my chest, I kick and send Silas flying into the back of Daren's father. The green dome flickers out of existence as Daren's magic blasts the two remaining Board members who are tumbling through the air.

Astara is on top of Silas without a pause, Daren following her and jumping his father. Tenebris is helping them both, his jaws locking on flying limbs. He shakes his head, probably hoping to rip them off whatever body they are connected to. All the while, Soren hovers behind them waiting for an opening. Zoltan lifts me off the ground and tucks me to his side. I can feel my own rage radiating out of him, too. His is misplaced, but I can't tell him now that Soren was the one tugging and clawing on the bond. The Fae knows what Titans Roberti is hoping to unleash, and if he imprisoned them once, I have to hope he can do it again if it comes to it.

Astara sinks her fangs in Silas's throat, ripping her head back and almost decapitating the old fart. Soren darts in and slaps his bleeding palm to the gash on the side of her face, the female gasping from the magic. Zoltan's arms pull me closer, but I'm not sure if it's to comfort me or himself.

Daren hesitates.

The young mage holds his hand above his father's heart, and I know exactly how he feels. My brother's face comes to the front of my mind, bringing more bile that burns like acid to the back of my throat. For the first time since I've met him, the Fae does the first thing to show he has compassion. He sinks his hand in the chest of the old mage, tearing out his heart. The organ pulses in Soren's hand twice before the Fae squishes it to a pulp, his other palm wrapping around the back of Daren's neck.

My gaze finds Soren watching me, not Daren.

So, it wasn't compassion. He is mimicking it on my behalf.

"I can feel the magic taking hold in all three of them." Zoltan's deep voice is shaking my insides. "Mostly from Astara."

"He knows which Titans are being freed." I don't look away from the Fae.

"No one will be freed," Zoltan retorts, and Soren nods in acknowledgment.

Why don't I feel better now that the jerks who made me kill my brother are dead? Shouldn't I feel at least lighter because they won't hurt anyone else again? As if reading my mind, Soren glides closer, wiping his bloody hand on his silky pants. My spine snaps straight from his nearness as I eye him warily.

"They will not be freed," he repeats Zoltan's words. "As soon as the magic adjusts to their bodies we go hunting."

My heart jumps at the prospect of killing Roberti. Now that's one murder I can get behind. Pretending I'm calm and collected doesn't fool Soren or Zoltan. The Fae chuckles and his dragon eyes glitter in amusement.

"So blood thirsty, youn—Francesca." Catching himself, he uses my name instead of calling me young dragon.

My heartbeat trips over itself when I flick a look over Soren's shoulder and see Fenrir leaning on the wall staring at me. His face is unreadable, but uneasiness gnaws at my gut. I blink and he is gone like he was never there. There is a lot to talk about with Fenrir, but it'll have to wait. More important things are in order. Speaking of which.

"I need a shower to remove all the evidence that tonight happened." Taking hold of Zoltan's forearm, I use him as a shield.

"And after you rest?' Soren, ever the practical, reads my agreement loud and clear in my gaze.

"After I rest ..."—Tilting my head back, I stare at Zoltan's beautiful face and realize there is nothing I won't do for this male, except stay out of the upcoming battle. His clenched jaw confirms he knows it too. "We hunt."

Roberti will regret the day he was born.

vinci-books.com/ignited

Their veins are ice. My blood is fire. Let's see who burns first.

The Dragon Blood's awake. The Titans are coming. And fate just handed me the match.

I thought love was my choice—but now it might be our greatest weapon… or our downfall.

Turn the page for a free preview…

Ignited: Chapter One

When things go from bad to worse, expecting a horrible scenario in which the Fates will take advantage and kick you while you're down is kind of a given. Being brought to your knees too many times to count is never enough, be it as a human or a supernatural. In this it seems we have too much in common with our very mortal cohabitants in this world. It's been a constant occurrence in my life, so why fool myself otherwise? With that in mind, I stick to my proven method of distracting myself. In this case, it's not turning into a couch potato and stuffing my face with chocolate and food until I wind up in a coma.

To some, the chirping of birds, gurgling springs, or even soft whispers of the wind through the trees may be sounds that will relax them and bring a smile to their face. To others, like myself, the pained groan when Zoltan's body hits the floor after I sweep his feet under him is something that makes my heart sing.

A grin stretches my lips so high my cheeks hurt from it.

"Better." Huffing arrogantly like he didn't just eat the dust off the floor, he jumps on his feet.

"Better?" Slamming both fists on my hips, I glare at him. "You mean, 'that was awesome Franky. I absolutely did not see it coming.'"

"Calm down. You need to stop being cocky." Typical Zoltan, he is oblivious to the hole he is digging for himself. Who in their right mind will tell a female to calm down when there is steam coming out of her ears? A male, that's who. "Of course I saw it coming, I was just hoping that you would follow through and make sure I didn't get up. At the moment I could attack you right back, and then you've wasted all your energy for just one solid hit."

"You want me to kill you?"

"I need you to stop holding back, Francesca."

"It doesn't work that way, you jerk. You are helping me gain more control. Me making you bleed or hurting you doesn't show control at all. It just means I go all nuts again."

"I am immortal, so if it takes me bleeding to ensure I won't be worried about you when the time comes, I'm willing to have my blood spilled. Stop holding back." The words are punctuated with a stubborn tilt of his chin.

From the very beginning, Zoltan has been adamant about making sure I'm trained properly to face whatever Roberti throws at us—or anyone else for that matter. That damn bond turned him into an unbearable creature breathing down my neck and constantly pushing me harder. The difference with then and now is simple: he has stopped flirting, and he's no longer his arrogant self. Even the perpetual smirk is missing from his lips. Clinging to what-ever tunnel vision that has him stuck in his head, he is hell bent on me training daily until I can barely twitch a finger. By the time we are through, I want to crawl back to my room. Eyeing him through slanted lids, my stomach somersaults when the realization hits me like a brick. It's right there in the hard set of his jaw, the clenching of his fists, and the stiff set of his shoulders. How have I never noticed it before?

He is afraid.

For me …

"Where is this coming from, Zoltan?" With my heart drumming against my ribcage, I take a step closer and reach for his face. The sharp lines of his firmly pressed lips and clenched jaw soften as he nuzzles his face in my palm. "This past week, I can't remember the last time you've pissed me off with your smirking. From the time I wake up until I pass out on the pillow from exhaustion, you are like a machine with just one setting. Tiring me to death is your mission in life."

Zoltan's lips part in a sigh and his stiff shoulders slump slightly, while his gaze searches my face. I wait him out, not daring to twitch a muscle while my heart is trying to punch a hole in my throat. It's unnerving seeing him afraid. He was calm and unperturbed when hunters had poisoned blades under his throat. I realize I'm counting on him always being like that, being my rock when everything around me is falling apart. When he starts lowering his mouth closer to mine, my face tilts up on its own, like a flower searching for the sun. I can feel his breath tickling my lips and it sends a frenzy of butterflies through my stomach.

"I can try to train with her if it'll be easier."

Jerking away from Zoltan, my head snaps to Soren. Leaning a shoulder on the wall with one ankle crossed over the other, he has been watching us like some creep for who knows how long. His silky pants shimmer like liquid silver down his legs where his bare feet poke out under them. And would it kill him to put on a damn shirt? Platinum hair frames his perfect face with lips curled slightly at the edges, making him look like he knows something we don't. His golden eyes twinkle full of mischief while reflecting the flames flickering around the room.

The Dragon Blood is as sneaky as a freaking cat, catching us all unaware. You never know when he is going to pop up out of nowhere. I stifle my frustration so I don't hurt his feelings, but Zoltan doesn't suffer from being nice like that. The Daywalker turns his overwhelming glare at the object of his anger, his emotions descending over the three of us like a dark cloud. The training room is large enough to fit an army of us in it at the same time, yet all the oxygen gets sucked out like we are being vacuum sealed.

"I thought I should offer." Lifting both hands palms up, Soren looks as innocent as a child, though his voice echoing through the almost-empty space and bouncing off the walls all seductive-like and full of humor suggests otherwise.

"That's nice of you." Elbowing Zoltan until I hear him grunt, I smile tightly at Soren.

"He will continue taking advantage of your kindness, Francesca. How is it you can't see that?" Stepping slightly in front of me, Zoltan doesn't look away from the ancient Fae. For a moment, it's almost as if he is staring at the enemy.

"He can hear you." Hissing at his back, I poke him for emphasis. "It's time to take a break anyway." Speaking much louder, I sidestep the territorial vampire and head for Soren, wincing when all my muscles protest at the movement.

I can feel Zoltan's heat at my back.

"How are things going with the others?" When I'm a foot away from the Dragon Blood, a shiver crawls up my spine when Zoltan's shadow falls over Soren and sharpens his high cheekbones. "Are they acclimating to their powers yet? When can we see them?" The intent, unreadable look in his eyes makes me blabber like a fool.

"Meh, they are being childish." Flicking his wrist as if he's chasing flies, his lips twist with displeasure. "They keep fighting fate. No one wins against it, it just makes everyone miserable. What is the saying?" Tilting his head left and right, he snaps his fingers with a broad smile. "If you can't beat them, join them. That is all they need to do."

Unable to help myself, I smile right back at him. "Look at you picking up all the modern sayings. Soon enough you'll start saying dude." A giggle escapes me at the humor dancing in the ancient Fae's eyes.

"Did I do well?" The simple question is so full of eagerness that the smile slips from my lips.

"What?"

"Isn't that what you want, Francesca?" My confusion must be clear because a line forms between his perfect brows puckering them up. "For me to fit in the modern times, your time. Is that not what you want?"

The short hairs on the back of my neck stand on end when a feral growl comes from deep in Zoltan's chest.

"No." Flinching when I snap at him, I blow out a breath, my hands clenching at my sides. "It's not what I want, Soren. It's what *you* want. That's what you should do."

"Is it?" New interest sparkles in his gaze. He is totally ignoring Zoltan's presence and all his focus is centered on me. "I believe you want me to fit in with the rest of them. You are uneasy when I'm being myself."

"I'm uneasy when you are being creepy as fuck, like right now for example." A nervous laugh is pushed through my lips and I subtly slide to my right, blocking Zoltan from snatching the Fae by the throat. "And stop provoking Zoltan. It's annoying."

"I do no such thing, I assure you." The cheeky smile says he is doing exactly that and enjoying the crap out if it, too. "The mighty Zoltan is just unsure how to deal with his own emotions, as well as how to keep a female like you by his side. I'm not the only one that needs to come to terms with modern times, it seems."

A fist zooms past my head, ruffling the short hairs that have escaped my braid. I jump back a step when Zoltan's hand punches a hole through the wall an inch from Soren's face. The Fae doesn't bat an eye at the aggressive display, but I'm fighting a panic attack while I try to swallow my heart from my throat so it pushes back to my chest. It's beating wildly at the roof of my mouth and my eyes are about to pop out of their sockets. The vampire's body is vibrating and growing in front of me, his shoulders bunching and his muscles jumping. Zoltan's powers are blasting out as if I have placed my face in front of a fire, and my eyes tear up from the stinging of my skin, though it takes my brain a long moment to come online.

"Knock it off, both of you." Stepping between them like a referee, I slap a hand on each of their chests to separate them. "We have enough shit to deal with already. The last thing we need is to be biting each other's heads off."

A deep rumble followed by a predatory cry comes from the open doorway, freezing the blood in my veins. Tenebris bares his sharp teeth at both males, his tail lashing behind him in agitation. With his ears pinned to the back of his head, he glowers at them while his whiskers tremble on his curled upper lip. With paws as wide as my head, he pads closer until he reaches me and presses the left one on top of my foot. The action is loud and clear, a dare for them to continue messing with me and they'll both end up with his jaw clamped around their neck.

My hand grabs hold of the fur on his neck on instinct, my fingers sinking into the smooth, silky strands. As always, Tenebris rubs his cheek on my thigh, acknowledging the weird connection we formed what feels like a lifetime ago. From the first time I saw him, he hasn't left my side if he can help it.

"You are right, young dragon." Inclining his head regally, Soren straightens and pushes off the wall. "I apologize for causing you distress. It's all just good fun for me. I see now that I was mistaken."

Narrowing my eyes at his face, I say nothing. If I've learned anything about Soren, it's that he is always up to no good. Causing trouble like a toddler set loose in a toy store, the ancient Fae loves playing games with all of us. It's not like I'm special, either, because he does the same to all of my friends, too.

"I mean it, Soren." Stabbing my forefinger to the center of his chest, I emphasize each word with a new poke. "Stop. Making. Trouble."

"As you wish." The fond smile on his face makes me feel like an ass. I push the feeling away because I know it's just one of his ways to get what he wants.

Damn manipulative Fae.

"And what's wrong with you?" I turn to Tenebris when he starts nudging me with his whole body, guiding me forcefully toward the door.

An angry hiss is the answer to my glare.

"Let's see what made him come get you." Taking hold of my hand, Zoltan doesn't wait for and answer, nor does he hesitate for the Dragon Blood we are leaving behind. I have to walk faster to keep up with his pace.

"Would it be too much to ask for one day without any drama in this place?" Huffing, I look over my shoulder to see Soren following behind us at a slower pace. "Well, come on. No need to stay away from us, just don't be an ass."

"I shall try, dràgon òg." Closing the space between us, Soren's musical lilt when he speaks the ancient language spreads warmth through my chest.

He looks too willing to do what he is being told.

It doesn't sit well with me, but I let Zoltan guide me through the hallways anyways as we follow Tenebris to whatever needs our attention. There is an insistent feeling at the back of my mind that a shitstorm is coming, but I can't really put my finger on it. Once again, I glance at Soren over my shoulder.

If I learned one thing for sure, it's that when a Fae is willing to play by your rules, you better start reading the fine print real fast.

Ignited: Chapter Two

"Will you stop staring?" Zoltan murmurs from behind me, looming over my shoulders while I lean on the wall stretching my neck like a giraffe to get a better look.

"You can't be serious. Did you see him?" Whisper-yelling, I don't even turn to give him *THE* look. "What in all the worlds happened to him?"

Fenrir and Leo are leaning close to each other face to face, whispering low enough that if not for staring at their lips and seeing them move, I may think they're about to kiss. It looks hot as fuck, but that's not what I'm supposed to be paying attention to. It's not why I'm glued to the wall impersonating Soren the creep.

No, It's Fenrir.

The illusion that makes the Fae who he is, or as I know him mostly, is gone. No more androgynous face, or platinum blonde hair. Even the vibe coming off him is no longer soft, calm, and collected. Instead, sharp features with cheekbones that will cut through stone are framed by a curtain of midnight black hair reaching down to his waist, shining like oil under the flickering flames and the streaming moonlight coming through the windows.

Deep red runes form thin lines pulsing softly across his jaw, forehead, and neck, disappearing under the collar of his black t-shirt. He doesn't look like the male I know. Not like the one I called friend in any case. And it's not so much his changed appearance that freaks the hell out of me, and obviously Tenebris too since he brought us here to show me this. It's the energy coming from Fenrir and the way he holds himself.

He looks primal.

Scary even.

"You think Roberti got to him and messed him up?" Glancing at Zoltan is a bad idea.

My self-appointed babysitter is giving me a cocked-eyebrow look, calling me insane without opening his mouth. Not wanting to talk in case I'm overheard, I wave my hand in the direction of the two males who are conversing silently but just a little too enthusiastically, fast enough to make my wrist pop like a firecracker in the silent hallway.

My heart stops.

So did everyone else's, including the two I am spying on.

"Oh hey." Acting like I'm coincidently coming from around the corner, I grin at Fenrir and Leo, pretending I just noticed them. "You have to help me and keep Zoltan away from me. He is trying to kill me with his training. Did you hear that pop? That was from my joints and all thanks to the jerk." For some stupid reason I keep spewing words. Probably because I'm a moron and completely unable to close my mouth to stop the disaster I can clearly see coming. "How are you doing, pup? Hanging in there, huh? Oh, hey Fenrir, long time no see." To my horror, I giggle too, which makes both of them squint at me.

"You should stop. Honestly, it would actually be painful to watch you continue." Leo grins at my stupidity, and I cringe seeing the laughter he is suppressing.

"I don't know what you're talking about." Giving it a last-ditch effort, I even try to look confused.

Even Zoltan chuckles at that.

I glare at him since he has decided to stand far enough away that I can't elbow him.

The vampire is learning my tricks.

"I believe he is referring to your spying skills, dràgon òg," Soren ever-the-helpful chirps from behind me, and I grind my teeth at his words.

At this, Fenrir's lips twitch at the corners, although the haunted look in his white-on-black eyes takes my breath away. My ribs tighten painfully and prevent me from taking a full breath. I haven't seen the Fae since Leo, Daren, and Astara took over the Order of the Academy. What I'm looking at now is an entirely different person, and there's no trace of my friend and confidante.

"Fenrir ..." my voice trails off when he lifts a hand to stop me from saying anything else.

"It's a long story." Soren snorts indignantly at Fenrir's comment from behind me, but the Fae ignores him. "And I will explain everything when I can. Right now, I need Leo's help and a promise from all of you that whoever comes back with him to Sienna will be protected."

"Human?" Zoltan turns all business, his arms folding across his chest in reaction to an unknown threat to what he considers his domain. If he keeps this territorial bullshit up, I honestly won't be surprised if he starts pissing on everything.

"Half bloods ..." My spine snaps to attention hearing that. "I can't be sure how many will be coming, but some

194

might be just like the mother and two half bloods that Leo brought not long ago." Running a hand through his hair in frustration, Fenrir huffs out a heavy sigh. "Myst made a deal with a human to have them saved from the hunter's compounds."

"And we trust this human?" I really want to punch Zoltan for the question, because as soon as I hear half bloods, I want to run head first and get them out myself. I understand his worry too, so I bite on the inside of my mouth to keep it shut.

"I do." My body jerks as if Fenrir has slapped me.

"You trust humans?" I couldn't keep quiet any longer. Out of all of us, Fenrir is the one who looks down his nose at everyone, including some supernaturals.

"I trust that human. Not *humans*, Drake."

"Oh, we are back to Drake now. Got it." For some reason it rubs me wrong that he is distancing himself. I've done nothing to deserve it, which makes it an even more bitter pill to swallow. "Anyway"—Cutting off whatever he was going to say to that, I turn to Leo—"what can we do to help?"

"Nothing now until we know more about this. I will go meet with the human first." Scrubbing at the back of his neck, Leo peers at Zoltan with his lips pressed in a firm line. "You okay with that? I don't think I have the strength right now to deal with newcomers while I keep trying to control the influx of powers that continue to hit me from the academy and having to worry about fighting you if it comes to that."

"Why would he fight you?" Frowning I turn from Leo to Zoltan. "Why would you fight him?"

"He allowed himself a full transformation," Soren answers, while a muscle keeps pulsing in Zoltan's clenched jaw. "The territorial instincts are still too strong and he can't keep them under control. Not yet. It's what happens when you ignore or refuse your nature for too long." My eyes follow Soren's hand when he reaches up and rubs at the center of his chest absentmindedly. "Isn't that correct, Rìgh fuil?"

"What did you call him?" I have to remind myself that Soren can snap my neck with a flick of his wrist, otherwise I may slap him for constantly speaking in tongues.

"Blood King." An intent gleam enters Soren's gaze while he stares at Zoltan, as if he's daring him to dispute him or say something to contradict him. "Isn't that what you are, Zoltan?"

"We will take anyone the human brings to the portal and protect them." Turning his back to the Dragon Blood, Zoltan answers Leo. He is a bigger person than me. If looks can kill, Soren would be ashes right now based on the glare I pin him with. "As long as Francesca is nowhere near them, you will have no problem with me. Just keep them out of sight for now."

"I can help protect them, too." Jumping in their conversation, I lean heavily on Tenebris so I can see around Zoltan. "Wouldn't they be safer here with all of us? Let's not forget we still don't know if we have more moles telling Roberti our every move."

"As much as I would love to fight beside you, Drake, and antagonize Zoltan every chance I get at the same time, I don't think that's a smart idea. Not right now." One side of Leo's mouth curls, and it softens the sting of his words. It doesn't feel nice to be excluded.

"The two of you should talk," Fenrir says almost under his breath while he darts glances at Soren. "Don't do what I did." His white-on-black eyes lock on Zoltan and some unspoken understanding flows between them.

I want to ask a hundred questions but keep quiet, diverting my attention from them by gliding a hand over the panther's back. A deep purr vibrates through my palm all the way up to my elbow, and I look down at Tenebris. His keen, bright green eyes flick between all of us, his intelligence and cunning raising goosebumps over my arms.

"I must go back across the portal." Fenrir rolls his shoulders as if uncomfortable for being here with us. "If you need me, I will come ... if I can. Do not hold it against me if I'm otherwise occupied."

"Your loyalty has never been a question, old friend." Clasping the Fae's forearm, Zoltan slaps him on the back. "Do what you need to do. If you need our help, all you have to do is ask."

"This feels like a goodbye." Panic surges through me and I snatch Fenrir's arm in a tight grip, my nails digging into his skin. "Why does this feel like a goodbye? Is it me? Did I make you not want to be here?"

Old triggers rear their ugly head, choking me. *Half blood, unworthy, abomination, unwanted ... not enough, not enough, not enough ...* Words scream on repeat in my mind and silence everything else.

"Franky." I snap out of my downward spiral when Fenrir shakes me by the shoulders hard enough to make Tenebris snap his jaws a hairsbreadth away from his hand in warning. "You are not at fault for anything. Myst needs me, and I have denied myself long enough what I knew in my heart to be true."

"Oh ..." Blinking stupidly at him, I have to wait for the panic to subside so I can speak. Seeing Zoltan forcibly keeping himself from throwing the Fae off me clears the doubts that were trying to choke me as well. "I knew there was something between the two of you." Happiness warms my insides and I give Fenrir a big smile. "I'm not gonna say I won't miss having you around, Fenrir. I'll have no one to pick on."

Leo clears his throat loudly and my smile wobbles.

"The mutt will have to deal with all my glorious attitude now." If I'm blinking fast, it has nothing to do with the prickling tears at the back of my eyes. It's from the flickering flames. Right, that's the reason for sure.

"You cannot leave." There is no argument left when Soren speaks from behind me. "You made an oath."

"And you'll watch me break it, seann dràgon." Squaring his shoulders, the Fae glowers at Soren. "You can try to stop me, but I will not let you kill me easy."

"No one is killing anyone." Whirling on Soren, I grab his upper arm and shake him as if that will make him to stop being a jerk. He doesn't move an inch, but his eyes snap to my hand that is wrapped around his bicep. "You said it yourself: no one wins against the Fates. Stop being an ass or I'll castrate you."

I see Leo wince from the corner of my eye and Zoltan's eyebrows crawl up his forehead.

"Go, Fenrir. Say hi to Myst for me." Not taking my gaze away from Soren, I swallow the lump in my throat. "And don't be a stranger, okay?"

Not caring about the angry Dragon Blood, Fenrir turns me and wraps me up in a bone crushing hug. I cling to his shirt, grinding my teeth to stop the sob that's trying to escape me. With a kiss pressed on my forehead, he takes one step, then another before he spins on his heel and walks away. I keep looking at his back until it disappears out of sight.

"I'll come if you need me." Calling after him, my voice echoes off the high walls and ceilings.

"I know." I can hear him answer, but I wonder if I am just imagining it.

"He will be back." Zoltan comes behind me, his body enveloping mind as I lean the back of my head to his chest.

"Why is it that I don't believe you?"

He doesn't answer, and I'm grateful he is not trying to lie to me. There was a finality in Fenrir's hug that squeezed my heart until it felt like it would explode. I've always been on my own, even when Daren acted like he was there for me. Fenrir was the first true friend I had and watching him walk away feels like something inside me is breaking with no hope of repair. A chill spreads through me making me shiver in Zoltan's arms. Not even the heat of his body can warm me.

"It's the oath being broken," Soren spits in disgust.

"Huh?" My mind reeling, I turn absentmindedly toward him.

"That emptiness and ice you feel." His face twisted in anger, the Dragon Blood glares at the place where Fenrir disappeared. "It's the oath being broken."

"And you know this how?" Bile burns the back of my throat.

"He bound the two of you with the oath, and he can feel it break, too," Zoltan murmurs in my hair as he presses a kiss to the top of my head.

"I have no idea what any of you are talking about."

"It's time we have a talk." Zoltan sounds calm, but his heart is trying to punch a hole through his chest and my back.

"I will come for this talk as well." Soren juts his chin stubbornly.

I say nothing, still feeling raw from the knowledge that Fenrir left us for good. Zoltan tucks me under his arm, nodding at Leo as we walk past him. The alpha squeezes my arm in comfort but releases it too soon for my liking, and then we are gone.

I wish I can say the same about the ancient Dragon Blood following right behind me.

Soren is proving to be a bigger problem than I ever anticipated.

Grab your copy…
vinci-books.com/ignited

About the Author

Maya Daniels, USA Today Bestselling and multi-award-winning supernatural suspense author, is a fun-loving woman with many talents.

She traveled the world, gaining life experiences that helped her career as an investigative journalist, as well as her storytelling. Maya writes compelling tales of magic, mythical creatures, loyalty, and life-changing friendships with snarky female characters—much like herself.

Her travels have taken her to Europe, Africa, Asia, Australia, and America. Born with her feet in motion, she currently resides in Ohio, spinning her next epic story that you will not want to put down.

Her biggest 'sins' are her love of chocolate and coffee—through an IV drip! One to never sit still, Maya practices Reiki healing, different types of martial arts, reads about the arcane, talks to furry creatures more than humans, picks up a sledgehammer for home improvement, and travels with her fated mate, seeking her own adventures.